"This time will b[e] Brittany."

"What if it isn't?"

"You'll find a way. I know you. You're... tenacious." Mason checked to make sure Noah was nearby. His son was running toward the trees. "Hey, slow down, buckaroo."

"I'm gonna find us the biggest tree, Daddy!"

"Rule number one. It needs to fit in our house."

Brittany's laugh filled the air. She was gazing up at the sky. Her delight made Mason halt in his tracks. His pulse raced out of control, and it annoyed him. Because he didn't get all jittery around women. Not anymore.

Brittany raised her leg, bent it and did some sort of spinning move. Right there in the snow under the blue sky.

She was joyous and full of life. She took Mason's breath away. Brittany was tropical sun on his face after a cold winter. She was fireworks on the Fourth of July.

She was pure excitement to him. Always had been...

Jill Kemerer writes novels with love, humor and faith. Besides spoiling her mini dachshund and keeping up with her busy kids, Jill reads stacks of books, lives for her morning coffee and gushes over fluffy animals. She resides in Ohio with her husband and two children. Jill loves connecting with readers, so please visit her website, jillkemerer.com, or contact her at PO Box 2802, Whitehouse, OH 43571.

Books by Jill Kemerer

Love Inspired

Wyoming Sweethearts

Her Cowboy Till Christmas

Wyoming Cowboys

The Rancher's Mistletoe Bride
Reunited with the Bull Rider
Wyoming Christmas Quadruplets
His Wyoming Baby Blessing

Small-Town Bachelor
Unexpected Family
Her Small-Town Romance
Yuletide Redemption
Hometown Hero's Redemption

Visit the Author Profile page at Harlequin.com for more titles.

Her Cowboy
Till Christmas

Jill Kemerer

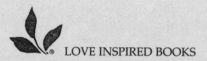

LOVE INSPIRED BOOKS

Recycling programs
for this product may
not exist in your area.

ISBN-13: 978-1-335-47959-4

Her Cowboy Till Christmas

www.Harlequin.com

Printed in U.S.A.

For he that is mighty hath done to me great things; and holy is his name.
—*Luke* 1:49

To Constance Phillips, my dear friend, favorite coffee date and writing buddy. I'm so thankful you invited me to join you for writing sessions at the coffee shop back when we first met. Look how far we've come!

And to all of the members of Maumee Valley Romance Authors, Inc. We've helped each other through ups and downs, shed a few tears, and educated and encouraged each other. I'm thankful for you.

Chapter One

It was going to be another lonely Christmas.

Mason Fanning tripped over a toy bulldozer, and his foot landed on an action figure. *Oof!* Hopping on the other foot, he winced until the sharp pain subsided. His three-year-old son, Noah, was having pizza and watching a Disney movie with Grandma and Grandpa Page like he did most Friday nights. Which left Mason alone, picking up toys and contemplating what to do with himself. The snowy December evening on his cattle ranch near Rendezvous, Wyoming, was ideal for sitting in front of a fire and watching a Christmas movie the way he and Mia used to. But without her in his arms, what would be the point?

Mia was gone.

He missed her. Three years had passed, and it still seemed like her funeral happened yesterday. He missed Ma and Pops, the grandparents who'd raised him, too. He hadn't felt this alone in a long time.

Mason snatched up the remaining toys and threw them into a basket. It was stupid to indulge in a pity party when he'd been blessed with more than most. Sure, the medical bills Mia left behind put a huge dent in his budget each month, but eventually he'd get the ranch churning out profits again. He'd leave a legacy to pass down to Noah, the way his grandparents had left Fanning Ranch to him.

A knock on the door startled him. No one ever stopped by on Friday nights.

Unless…

The emails and calls he'd been getting from Brittany Green came to mind. He hadn't answered them. He had nothing to say to her. And since it had been a decade since he'd seen her, the thought of her showing up was laughable, anyhow.

He strode to the entryway. Opened the door.

Snowflakes and familiar ocean-blue eyes greeted him.

Brittany stood there the way she had a million times during their childhood. Her hair was blonder than he remembered. Must have been all the California sunshine. Wearing jeans, a long puffy coat and tall boots, she was still the petite dancer he'd spent every waking minute with each summer growing up.

It had been ten years since their final summer together, and the anger still burned.

He shifted his attention to the man next to her. The world spun. *Impossible!* The man looked *exactly* like him. They could have been the same person. He braced his hand against the door frame.

"Mason?" Brittany stepped forward and touched his arm. He shook it off as if it were a scorpion. "Are you okay?"

His brain scrambled to come up with anything that made sense. Nothing did. Was this a practical joke? Who was this guy? How could they look so much alike?

And why was he with Brittany?

"Why are you here?" Mason's voice was low, gruff.

Her long dark lashes dipped briefly, then revealed

eyes swimming with sympathy. "I'm sorry. You look like you're in shock."

"Is this some kind of prank? Did you find an actor to impersonate me or something?" He knew he sounded unhinged, but why was she with this guy? This…this… eerie imitation of him?

"Why don't we go inside?" She motioned to the open doorway.

He didn't want her in his home. Didn't want to have to scrub away the memory later. But—he glanced at his spitting image—someone had some explaining to do.

"Make it quick." Against his better judgment, he shifted sideways to let them in.

"Ryder Fanning." The man's face had drained of color, but he stepped forward and held out his hand. "I believe I'm your twin."

Twin? *Twin?* He could *not* have a twin. Ma and Pops would have known about a sibling. They would have told him.

"I'm an only child." Mason clenched his jaw.

"So am I." Ryder's brown eyes, the same caramel shade as his own, had nothing to hide. "At least, I thought I was until I met Brittany."

"Come on," Brittany said, gesturing to them both. "This will be easier to figure out sitting down."

He wanted to escort her pretty five-foot-two-inch frame outside, slam the door shut and enjoy the satisfaction of hurting her the way she'd hurt him, but Ryder being here complicated things. Mason let out a *humph*, then jerked his chin for Ryder to enter. Hurt and irritation flashed in the man's eyes, but he moved with an easy, familiar gait into the house.

It was like watching a video of himself.

Brittany made herself right at home at the kitchen

table, and Mason resented it more than he thought possible. Sure, she'd been here countless times when she'd spent summers down the road with her grandmother Nan. But this was *his* table.

Mia's table.

Brittany didn't belong here.

As Ryder folded his sculpted frame onto the chair across from her, Mason sat and crossed his arms over his chest. "Someone had better start talking."

Ryder and Brittany exchanged glances.

"Two weeks ago, I was at my favorite coffee shop." She gestured with her hands as she talked, and those blue eyes ebbed and flowed with expressiveness. "I was mentally choreographing a solo for Kelly Jo, one of my best teen dancers—you really have to see this girl move, she's amazing—and I grabbed my coffee and turned to leave. Well, Ryder was right behind me." She blinked and shrugged. "I freaked out a little and, what do you know, I splashed coffee onto my white sweatshirt. As I was dabbing at it, I couldn't take my eyes off him. I... I thought it was you."

Brittany hadn't changed. She always took the scenic route when telling a story. Her voice had wavered at the end. The thought of running into him had obviously bothered her.

Good. It should.

Ryder cleared his throat. "She started asking me why I was in town and how I was, and she threw out names I'd never heard before. My confusion must have been obvious."

"You had the deer-in-headlights look, but that was to be expected." A tender smile lifted her lips, and Mason straightened. Were these two a couple? "I was a mess. Of all the times to be such a klutz... My words kept tripping over each other, and I don't know what I was doing rubbing the stains on my shirt."

"She kept saying 'Mason,' and it hit me she thought I was someone else." Ryder's shoulders and eyebrows rose in sync. His movements were so like his own, it made the hair on Mason's arms rise. "I told her she had the wrong guy. And I introduced myself."

"As soon as the last name came out of his mouth, I put it together." She shook her head slightly. "I could barely take it in. Still can't take it in, and it's not even happening to me. Mason, Ryder *is* your identical twin. All this time and you never even knew each other existed. I remember how much you wanted a brother. Now you have one!"

And there it was—the empathy that had always, always drawn him to her. He ground his teeth together. Once upon a time, he thought she knew him in a way no one else did. That she saw through to his essence and, more, that she liked what was there.

She'd been his first love, and the experience had hardened him. Her lies had helped him see what he really wanted in a woman, and he'd found a beautiful, honest, loyal best friend in Mia.

Mia was gone, and Brittany was here. Fury pulsed, hot and surging, but he forced himself to stay calm. Why was he so mad at Brittany, anyway? It had been ten years. They'd been teenagers. It wasn't as if he hadn't moved on with his life. He had.

And he'd lost. Again.

Always losing.

"Why'd you come?" He didn't miss the wariness that flashed in her eyes. "To flaunt your new boyfriend?" He regretted the words instantly. Couldn't take them back. Didn't know if he would have, anyway.

"You think we're…" Ryder pointed to Brittany and

back to himself. "Sorry if we gave you that impression. We aren't… It's not…. Well, I recently went through a difficult divorce, and I have three-year-old twin daughters to raise. I don't see myself dating anytime soon. Maybe ever."

Why relief sank into his limbs, he wouldn't examine. Another thing they had in common. Mason didn't see himself ever dating again, either. He'd had the love of his life. You only got that once.

He studied Ryder more closely. The resemblance was too much to take, kind of like staring into the sun. If this man *was* his twin—and there seemed to be no other reasonable explanation—his childhood had been built on a lie.

"Mason, I realize this is hard to accept, but I hope you'll get used to the idea. I mean, you have a brother. How cool is that?" Brittany's soft tone irritated him. As did the way she was trying to soothe him.

"You have no right to come in here and act like old times."

"Old times? I'm not… Aren't you the teensiest bit happy you have a brother?" Her face paled as she shook her head in disgust. "What happened to you?"

He closed his eyes briefly. What *had* happened to him?

The woman he'd cherished—the mother of his precious son—had died of cancer. That's what had happened.

And three years later, he still hadn't figured out how to move on.

"I can see this was a huge mistake." The legs of the chair scraped against the floor as Brittany rose to stand. Mason acted like she'd happily skipped up here in some warped attempt to see him suffer. The last place she wanted to be was Rendezvous. Santa Ana was her home.

She had people—mostly dance students—who genuinely liked her, who didn't look at her like she was a scab they'd picked off an old wound. "I'm sorry for putting you through this, Ryder."

She glanced at Mason to catch his reaction. The vein in his forehead throbbed.

Good.

She'd tried to call him. Emailed him again and again.

"Don't be. I asked you to come." The planes of Ryder's face were as sharp as his voice. He turned to Mason. "I figured she'd provide a buffer, introduce us. Maybe this *was* a mistake. I've always wanted a brother, but…"

Brittany could have filled in the rest. *Not if the brother is you, you big jerk.*

Since Ryder made no movement to leave, she stood behind her chair. The kitchen had changed since she'd last been here. She'd been eighteen then, and Mason's grandparents had still been alive. Since then, the oak cabinets had been painted white, new countertops gleamed and hardwood floors had replaced the cracked linoleum. The farmhouse charm was still there. Too bad it was the only charm left—Mason certainly had none.

The brothers were engaged in a charged stare-off. The tension made her rise on her tiptoes as they really studied each other for the first time. A look of wonder accompanied Mason's quick intake of breath. *Finally.* She slipped back into her seat. They'd been here for ten minutes, and it had taken Mason all ten to acknowledge reality.

"When is your birthday?" he asked Ryder.

"February 1." He leaned back, wariness in his eyes. "I was born in Colorado Springs. Raised in Billings, Montana."

Mason looked green.

Brittany resisted the urge to smirk. Did he really think

she'd have come all this way if Ryder wasn't the real thing?

Ryder tapped his fingernails on the table. "My parents were John and Lisa Fanning. Died in a head-on collision when I was a week old."

Mason flicked her a glance, and she could see his doubts disappearing. If she knew him at all, she'd say he wasn't quite ready to accept Ryder's word yet.

"Brittany could have told you all that." The bravado in Mason's voice was all bluff, and she could have called him out on it, but she stayed silent. This wasn't her battle. She had enough of those of her own right now.

"She could have, but she didn't," Ryder said. "Let's cut to the chase. We have the same parents, were born on the same day and in the same hospital. We look alike. I'm sure we have a lot of other things in common, too."

"Okay, so we're brothers." Mason ran his fingers through his hair. "Twins. Identical, clearly. How did we get separated?"

Ryder shrugged. "I wish I had the answer to that. My grandparents raised me, and they both died a while back. I don't have any other family—well, that I know of. And in the two weeks since finding out you existed, I haven't gotten up the nerve to dig into the whys."

"I didn't even know my other set of grandparents."

"Bo and Shirley Gatlin could be overbearing sometimes, but I think they couldn't handle the fact their daughter was gone. I hate to even tell you this, but they told me my other grandparents had died."

"I was told the same."

"Unbelievable," Ryder muttered under his breath.

The ticking of the hall clock broke up the ensuing silence. Part of Brittany was relieved Mason had accepted

Ryder was his twin. And part of her was still bristling over his rude reception.

"Look, I don't know where to take this. What do you want from me?" Mason's voice was gravelly.

"Want from you? Why would I want anything?" Ryder's face twisted in confusion. "I don't have any other family. Not anymore. I thought it would be great to have a brother. But maybe you don't feel the same."

Tension, thick and ripe, hung in the air. Brittany drew faint circles on the floor with the toe of her boot. What she wouldn't give to interpret the mood through dance. She mentally tucked away the sensation to choreograph a lyrical number later.

"I don't know what to think," Mason said.

"I see." Ryder stood, disappointment dripping off him like a hard rain. Brittany's heart broke a little. He'd come all this way and she was responsible. He hitched his chin to Mason. "I'm staying at the Mountain View Inn until Sunday afternoon. If you're interested in getting to know me, call me. If not, I guess this is goodbye."

Brittany scrambled to her feet. This wasn't how she'd pictured their meeting going. She wanted to talk sense into Mason, but his face said it all. The man had been born stubborn. He was allergic to change. Always had been.

But he'd also been reliable and trustworthy. Kind. A man of his word.

She opened her mouth to say something, to make it better, but what could she say? She barely knew him anymore. Ten years had changed him.

Ten years had changed her, too.

"Wait." Mason's voice softened. "I do want to get to know you. I'm just… This has been… Well, I think I need some time to process everything."

Ryder took out his wallet and handed Mason a business card. "Here's my cell number. Call me when you're ready. We'll figure out how to move forward." Then he walked out of the kitchen and back down the hall toward the entry.

Brittany turned to Mason. "I tried to contact you. I didn't come here to upset you."

His lips were drawn together in a tight line, and his brown eyes were hard, as hard as she'd ever seen them. Ryder was already halfway down the hall, so she pivoted to follow him. A framed photograph of Mason with his arm around a beautiful brunette holding a small baby mocked Brittany on the way out. Their love for each other radiated from the photo.

Her chest tightened, and she forced her legs forward. She'd had that kind of love for a few short months. But she'd been immature, scared of her feelings and unwilling to consider a future she hadn't planned out. Her dishonesty had cost her dearly.

The bottom line? She had always put her personal ambitions above love. She had then. She did now. Her relationships never lasted long, and she'd made peace with that.

Until she had her own dance studio, she wasn't diverting her energy to a here-today-gone-tomorrow romance. Making a name for herself in dance had been her goal ever since she was a child, and sometimes it felt further away than ever. She'd already surrendered her dreams of becoming a professional dancer. But she could still help other girls realize their dreams…if a bank would approve a line of credit so she could lease her own studio space.

Ryder held the front door open, and she nodded her thanks. She would enjoy this long-overdue visit with Nan, return to Santa Ana after Christmas and, in the meantime, pray the bank would call with the good news that her line of credit had been approved. A spot in a strip mall would be vacant in January. She had enough cash to pay for some of the renovations, but it would take several months to attract enough students to cover all her expenses.

If the bank turned her down, she'd have to reinvent herself, because she couldn't keep doing this anymore. Years of working odd jobs to pay off her student loans and save for the studio had taken their toll.

She hurried to Ryder's rental car and momentarily turned back to look at the house.

Mason glowered through the front window.

Well, at least she knew how he felt about her.

Some things never changed.

He'd handled that badly.

Mason collapsed onto the sofa and let his neck fall back into the cushion. What was he supposed to do now? He didn't know what upset him more—the fact he had an identical twin he'd never heard of or that Brittany had been the one to introduce them.

He'd been rotten to them both.

Well, what had they expected? If he would have had some warning, some time to process it...

He thought of all the emails and calls from Brittany he'd ignored.

He hadn't known she had anything important to tell him. Still, maybe he'd been wrong not to answer her. She hadn't exactly tried to contact him in ten years. Not once.

Which was fine. She hadn't really cared about him the way he'd cared about her. It probably should have affected how he felt about her grandmother, but it didn't. Nan— Ada Rhodes—lived a mile down the road from him in this secluded corner of Rendezvous. After Ma and Pops passed, Mason found himself checking on her more often.

She'd been slowing down for a while now, so for the past year he'd stopped in every weekday afternoon to see how she was doing and to feed the barn cats. On Saturdays, he and Noah popped over to her place to bring her groceries.

Nan was as close to a mother or grandmother as Mason had now. And he couldn't stand the thought of anything happening to her, either.

He pulled out the card Ryder had handed him, gave it a cursory glance and flicked it onto the end table.

Lies. So many lies.

Ma and Pops had to have known he had a twin brother. Not once had they mentioned it. Wouldn't they think he'd want to know he had a sibling?

An identical twin. Ryder.

His heart raced.

He wasn't ready to think about him. Not yet.

And what was with Brittany coming here to introduce them? Especially since he couldn't remember the last time she'd visited her own grandma. She didn't appreciate Nan. While she romped around California, Mason was the one taking care of her sweet grandmother. Not that he minded checking on Nan. He didn't.

The ticktock of the kitchen clock echoed through the house.

He'd give about anything to have Mia here right now. She'd know what to say. She'd rub his shoulders and ease the gnawing sensation gripping every muscle in his body.

He missed her so much.

The first year after she died, he'd strained to hear her laughter. He'd wake up in the dead of night, reach over to touch her and his lungs would seize when he realized he was alone. He'd find himself catching his breath as he entered the kitchen, knowing she wouldn't be there, but somehow expecting her to be rolling out dough for cinnamon buns. The second year after she died, his in-laws, Bill and Joanna Page, had begun to cling to him and Noah even more, and his memories of Mia had grown fuzzy. Last year, the third year, Mason could no longer hear the echoes of her gentle laugh. Worse, he was drowning under Bill's expectations of him. Mason itched to create a sliver of distance from his in-laws, and they were just as determined to keep him glued to their side.

His cell phone's loud ring made him jump. "Hello?"

"You're not going to believe this." His friend Gabby Stover managed Mountain View Inn, and every Tuesday night he met with her and his sister-in-law, Eden Page. They'd formed their own support group to deal with the tragedies they'd experienced. He and Eden were still trying to piece their lives back together after Mia's death, and Gabby's sister had recently died of a heart attack after giving birth to a baby girl. Gabby was now raising little Phoebe as her own daughter. Thankfully, Eden babysat Noah and Phoebe for him and Gabby while they worked. He didn't know what he'd do without them.

"I don't want you to freak out." Her words tumbled out quickly.

Gabby must be working tonight. It hadn't occurred to him to warn her Ryder was on his way to the inn.

"I already know. I have an identical twin." Saying the words out loud made them seem real. How had he made it twenty-nine years without knowing he had a twin? Maybe he'd better stop wondering and start coming up with a plan for what to do about his long-lost brother.

The sound of her gasp came through the line. "Why didn't you tell me?"

"I just found out myself. He stopped by."

"What do you mean he stopped by? How did he find

you? Did you know you had a twin? Why isn't he with you now?"

Sometimes Gabby was the bossy older sister he'd always wanted. Not tonight, though. "An old…er…friend of mine ran into him in California and figured we should meet."

"California? Who?"

"Brittany Green."

"Wait—Brittany? The name sounds familiar. Do I know her?" He could hear computer keys tapping in the background. "Couldn't she have called first?"

"She's Nan's granddaughter. And she did call. I didn't answer."

"Nan's…oh, that's right. Why wouldn't you answer? And I'm surprised you let Ryder come to the inn. Why is he staying here and not at your place?"

He suppressed a groan. Of course Gabby would assume he'd invited Ryder to stay. She was like that—welcoming to all. Well, not cowboys. She had an odd aversion to them.

"I didn't ask him." Should he have asked him to stay?

"Why not?"

"Seeing him was a shock. I needed time to process."

"No doubt. For what it's worth, he seems nice." A moment of silence stretched between them on the line. "You *are* going to talk to him more while he's here, right?"

Yes. But what if it opened a can of worms he'd rather be left shut? What else had Ma and Pops lied to him about? How much of his past was true and how much was false?

"I think so," he said.

"Good. This is your family. You should get to know him better."

"Yeah. It's a lot to take in." A lifetime of wanting a sibling pulled hard on his heart. What if he got to know—and love—his brother only to lose him the way he'd lost his grandparents and Mia? Nothing good stuck around his life for long.

Except Noah. Mason trusted God would always take care of his son.

"I'll pray about it, and you should, too." Muffled sounds came through the line. "Prepare yourself, though. Babs saw him on the way to his room and thought it was you. He set her straight."

A sinking sensation slid down to his stomach. Babs O'Rourke was the owner of Mountain View Inn and could only be described as a busybody. In her early seventies, she had flaming red hair, talked a mile a minute and noticed everything—and everyone—in Rendezvous. The entire town would know he had a twin before dawn.

"Can I let you go?" Gabby asked. "I'm being summoned."

"Sure. Talk to you later."

He got up and poured himself a glass of water. Gabby was right. He needed to pray. Between juggling single fatherhood and managing his ranch, he was full up on problems. This fall he'd had to make tough decisions about his cattle herd. The payment plan for Mia's medical bills didn't allow any wiggle room in his budget. Until he paid them off, he needed the ranch to bring in more income than it currently was.

And now this…

Maybe his tattered baby book would have some answers. Or the boxes of old photos in the attic might hold some clues.

One thing was certain—whatever he decided to do about Ryder, he'd be doing on his own. As far as he was concerned, he'd had enough of Brittany Green for another ten years.

Chapter Two

Rendezvous was a middle-of-nowhere town where dreams died. That's what her mother had always told her, anyway.

The next morning, Brittany slipped her feet into fuzzy slippers and padded into Nan's kitchen for a cup of coffee.

Rendezvous hadn't always been the dream killer her mother claimed. Until Brittany graduated high school, it had been more like a welcoming hug—a place to catch her breath each summer. But she couldn't deny her mom's words. One of her dreams had died here a decade ago. And the others had no shot at coming true in these parts. A small town in Wyoming wasn't the place to put together an elite competitive dance team, that was for sure.

California had been the right choice ten years ago.

The kitchen window revealed a pastel glow in the early dawn sky. After scooping grounds into a coffee filter, she filled the carafe with water and pressed the On button. Nan wasn't up yet. Strange. Her grandmother had always been an early riser. She must be more tired than usual.

Brittany had rearranged her schedule to spend two weeks here—just until after Christmas. It had been a long time since she'd been back. A year at least. Maybe two.

Had it been three years since she'd visited?

She listened for sounds of her grandmother. Silence. Maybe she should check on her.

She peeked into the bedroom where Nan slept peacefully. She looked…older, smaller than Brittany remembered. When had Nan gotten so frail?

Brittany used to call her every Sunday, but Nan's hearing wasn't the greatest, so she'd been skipping the calls to write letters instead.

She shouldn't have stayed away so long.

After closing the door carefully, she padded back to the living room. Gurgles from the coffee maker told her it wasn't finished brewing. Wrapping a blanket around her shoulders, she ticked through a mental list to make sure she hadn't forgotten anything back home.

It had been hard to juggle her schedule and finances to make this trip. For as long as she could remember, she'd been working three jobs. Besides the diner gig and freelance data entry work, she rented rehearsal space in an established studio to teach classes. The arrangement didn't allow her to hire more teachers, expand her class offerings or put together a competitive dance team, though. So far all but one bank had turned down her application for a line of credit to open a studio in Santa Ana's expensive market. She'd be hearing from them soon.

A window overlooked the porch of Nan's weathered one-story house. Jagged reddish mountains with thin, horizontal white stripes jutted in the distance. The snow-covered prairie seemed to whisper, and clumps of bare trees dotted it here and there.

This land was quiet, unforgiving—and breathtaking. Like Mason.

She'd fallen hard for him as a teen. Actually, she'd had

a crush on him for years. Not surprising, since they'd been inseparable every summer.

The minute she'd arrived in Rendezvous after graduating from high school, she knew something had changed in their relationship. The glint in Mason's eyes had set her heart pounding wildly. A sweet kiss had sealed it. The rest of the summer had been spent holding hands, hiking, hanging out, laughing and talking.

And the longer it went on, the guiltier she'd felt.

No one had known she had a boyfriend back home. For months she'd been hoping Parker would take the hint and end things with her, but he wasn't a take-the-hint kind of guy. She should have broken up with him before coming to Rendezvous.

Why hadn't she?

Because Mom had actually approved of him, and her mother never thought much of anything Brittany did.

Ancient history. She tossed the blanket off her shoulders. What was taking the coffee maker so long? And why was she thinking about that summer, anyhow? She must be in caffeine withdrawal.

But the memories kept coming. The final night here was seared in her memory like a scarlet *A*. On Nan's front porch, Mason had asked her to stay in Wyoming instead of going back to California. She'd stood there in silence trying to figure out how to explain. She was going to become a professional dancer. He *knew* she'd already been accepted into UCLA's dance program. How could she do those things in Rendezvous?

Then disaster had rolled up in a Porsche. Her boyfriend, Parker, sick of her avoiding his calls, had shown up at the worst possible time. Mason's face had said it all. He'd looked her in the eye and told her he never wanted to see her again. She'd never been so ashamed in her life. And she'd unintentionally made good on his wishes until yesterday.

The coffee maker rumbled. Finally. She returned to the kitchen, grabbed her favorite mug and poured herself a cup of joe, focusing on the good memories. Endless hours with Nan. Hugs and bedtime prayers. Failed summer reading plans and successful baking sessions. Feeling loved and cherished by her grandmother.

It really was good to be back.

Footsteps made her turn. Nan smiled, holding out her arms for a hug. Brittany embraced her, noting how thin her body was under the cotton nightgown and robe. "How did you sleep?"

"Good. It's wonderful to wake up to your smiling face."

"Want a cup of coffee?" Brittany turned to the counter.

"Yes, lots of sugar. Lots of cream."

"You got it." She found a container of store-bought pastries and put them and some chocolate chip cookies on a plate. Then she poured Nan a cup of coffee and settled in with her at the table.

"I'm sorry it's been so long since I've visited." She reached over and covered Nan's hand with her own. Her bony fingers felt fragile.

"Oh, honey, you're busy." Nan patted her hand. "No need to apologize. I would have come to California for Christmas, but I…" A lost expression flitted through her eyes.

Nan used to come visit for Christmas, but it had been a few years. Her vibrant grandmother was fading. How had she not picked up on it before?

"I've always wanted to spend Christmas here with all the snow." She just never could get the time off in the past.

"Plenty of snow here." Nan took a sip. "Did you try out for the dance team?"

Try out? She drew her eyebrows together. "Nan, I did try out in college, and I made the Spirit Squad my sophomore year. Don't you remember?"

A flicker of concern crossed Nan's face. "Oh, that's right. I remember you saying something about a dance team. I get my dates mixed up sometimes." She pushed the plate Brittany's way. "Cookie?"

"Yes, please." She selected one bursting with chocolate chips and bit into it. *Mmm...*

"Mason and Noah bring these every week. Have you seen the baby yet? He's a darling child."

"No, I haven't." The cookie suddenly tasted like ashes.

"And what about you?" Nan asked. "Are you thinking of marrying the banker?"

Banker? What banker? She couldn't mean Charles, could she? "Charles and I broke up a long time ago." Four years, if memory served her right.

"You did? I thought you'd marry him."

"Nope. We weren't meant to be." Within two months Charles had apparently decided she wasn't serious girlfriend material. He'd dumped her and started dating a marketing executive shortly after.

She sighed. The story of her dating life.

"Have you been feeling okay?"

Nan took the tiniest sip of her coffee, a faraway look in her eyes. "Yes, things are fine."

Things didn't seem all that fine. Maybe she was just forgetful since it was so early in the morning. Memory lapses were a normal sign of aging, weren't they?

"Mason will be here in a little while," Nan said. "You two can run off and play the way you used to every summer."

"Does Mason come here often?"

"Oh, yes." Her shoulders poked through her thin cotton robe. "That reminds me…what day is it?"

"It's Saturday." It didn't surprise her that Mason would stop by now and then. He'd always been fond of Nan. Brittany took another bite of cookie.

"Shopping day. I'd better make my list. You can go with him." Nan padded over to a kitchen drawer. She returned to the table with a pen in one hand and a small notebook in the other. With shaky movements, she wrote *milk*, *eggs* and *bread* on the list. Then she stared into space.

"Why don't you and I go to the store together?" Brittany asked. She and Ryder had flown into the nearest major airport, and together they'd driven to Rendezvous in his rental car. He was driving back to the airport tomorrow to catch his flight, and she figured she could borrow Nan's truck to get around during her stay. "I'll drive you to town if you don't mind me borrowing your truck."

"You can borrow it anytime. But Mason always does the shopping."

Always? When had Nan stopped doing her own shopping? No matter what Nan said, Brittany highly doubted Mason would stop by with her being there.

"He might not be over today."

Nan brightened. "Oh, no. He'll be here."

Nan had been confused about a few things this morning. Brittany hoped she was wrong about this, too.

But Mason was nothing if not dependable. Something told her she'd be seeing him sooner rather than later.

"Nan's!" Noah jumped up and down, clapping his hands. His brown eyes sparkled and his blond hair was mussed. His cheekbones were all Mia's. Mason wished she could see Noah now. "After cookies, we feed the kitties, Daddy."

Mason loved the kid's enthusiasm. His son loved Nan, and every day it was the same request—have a cookie, then feed the cats in Nan's barn. But after a sleepless night wrestling with the fact he had a twin and a frigid morning feeding and working the cattle, Mason had no plans to visit Nan, even if it was shopping day. Brittany could take care of it.

But would she? He raised his eyes to the ceiling. Probably not. She knew nothing about Nan's needs. And if Ryder was leaving tomorrow, Brittany would be heading out with him.

After the early-morning chores, Mason had called Ryder and invited him out to the ranch. Ryder was dealing with an unexpected work emergency but said he'd be over this afternoon.

Anticipation wound Mason up tighter than a lassoed calf. He was eager to learn more about his brother, to find out what else they had in common, but what if it poured gasoline on his happy childhood memories? He didn't want his entire past to go up in flames.

"We're not going to Nan's today." His shoulders tensed as he waited for the inevitable meltdown. He couldn't exactly tell his son the truth—that his ex-girlfriend had rattled his nerves and he'd rather jump in the ice-cold waters of Silver Rocks River than run into Brittany again.

"Yes we are, Daddy. We go to Nan's every day cuz we love her."

No tantrum? That was a first. His conscience whimpered at his own words being repeated back to him. He pulled on his cowboy boots. "That's right, but her granddaughter is in town visiting. We'll give them some space."

"But, Daddy, what about the kitties? And the food? We

have to buy Nan's food." Noah tried to step into his own small cowboy boot and almost fell over. "I don't wanna be on the naughty list."

"Why don't you sit next to me on the bench and pull on your boots, buckaroo?" He patted the bench. "And you won't be on the naughty list. Remember why we celebrate Christmas?"

"Jesus's birthday." He clutched the boots to his chest and hoisted himself onto the bench as one boot clattered to the ground. Mason picked it up and helped him tug it onto his foot. The other went on quickly. "But Nan'll miss me, Daddy."

"You'll see her Monday."

He screwed up his face, his chubby cheeks puffing out in confusion. "When's that?"

Mason held up two fingers. "In two days."

"Two days? No! Too long. I want Nan today!" His little face grew red.

"Noah," he warned, giving him a stern look. A text came through his phone. He almost groaned when he saw it was from his father-in-law, Bill.

What's this I hear about you having a twin? Joanna and I are coming over to discuss it.

Acid reflux burned his throat. Thanks to Babs, the news of Ryder had likely spread through town like the bubonic plague. Mason had already received several texts from locals. He'd ignored the phone calls. The thought of *discussing* the situation with Bill and Joanna right now gave him heartburn.

He didn't want to talk to anyone about Ryder until he'd had a chance to speak with him more in-depth. Figure out why on earth they were separated and how anyone could justify keeping them apart.

Without wasting a second, he texted Bill back.

I just found out myself. Noah and I are out shopping for Nan, and we have plans this afternoon. I'll fill you in later.

He slipped the phone into his pocket. If a few minutes in Brittany's presence was the price to pay for avoiding his in-laws, he'd pay it. He'd dealt with worse punishments in his life.

"Okay, buckaroo. We'll pop in to get Nan's list. But we aren't having cookies or checking on the cats because we don't want to interrupt her visit. We can buy a doughnut in town instead."

"With sprinkles?"

"You got it."

Five minutes later, Mason's truck rumbled up Nan's drive a mile down the road from his. The peace of the white prairie and distant mountains always made him say a silent prayer to thank God for letting this beautiful spot be his home. After parking, he got out of the truck, nudged his cowboy hat into place and unbuckled Noah from his car seat before setting him on the snow-covered ground. The boy took off running toward the front porch yelling, "Nan! I'm here!"

She opened the door and clapped as she bent to greet Noah. He took her by the hand and went inside. The sight of white-haired Nan in her saggy pants and embroidered sweatshirt holding hands with his little boy always made Mason smile.

He followed them into the entry, took off his hat and froze. Brittany stood only a few feet away, her blue eyes locked with his. He blinked away the connection. Noah had climbed onto a chair at Nan's table and was already helping himself to a cookie.

"We're here to get your list." Mason crossed over to give Nan a hug.

She patted his cheek, but confusion wrinkled her forehead. "List? Oh, right! Now where did I put it?" She began moving around the kitchen, then meandered down the hallway. Mason was used to it. She usually forgot where she put it and would find it a few minutes later.

"Who are you?" Noah peered up at Brittany.

"I'm Brittany. Nan is my grandma."

"She is?" Noah's mouth was full of a cookie. "I love Nan."

"I do, too."

"Can we go see the kitties, Daddy?"

"Not today. As soon as Nan finds the list, we have to head out." He held his breath, hoping Noah wouldn't throw a fit.

"Can I pwease see the kitties, Daddy? Pwease?"

"No." Mason craned his neck down the hallway. *Come on, Nan, find your list already!*

"I can take him out there for a minute." Brittany smiled at Noah.

"Yay!"

"I said no." It came out more harshly than he intended. But he didn't want her around his son at all.

"Mason, I forgot about the water softener," Nan called from the back of the house. "Do I need more salt?"

"Really, I don't mind." Brittany pushed her hair behind her ear. She wore black leggings and a long heather-gray sweatshirt with the word *Sunshine* written in cursive across the front. Her lack of makeup gave her a freshly scrubbed air. It reminded him of what she'd looked like as a teen and, unbidden, brought the warm feelings he'd had for her then with it.

"See, Daddy? She don't mind." Noah's big eyes brimmed with hope.

He sighed and gave them both a tight smile. "Okay. Just for a minute. But be careful and listen to Miss Brittany."

"I will!" His legs were already carrying him to the back door.

"Wait, Noah." The kid didn't even have his winter jacket on. "You have to wear your coat. Zipped."

Noah rushed back and let Mason bundle him up before taking off again. Brittany, who'd slipped her feet into boots, put her coat on and followed. The soft click of the door shutting told him they were gone.

Why would she have offered to take his kid? He'd been really rude to her last night. If it had been anyone else, he'd assume they were being kind. But he didn't know Brittany. Not anymore. Once upon a time he'd thought he'd known her, and he'd been wrong.

The door to the basement was through the kitchen, so he flipped on the light before tromping down the stairs. He lifted the lid to the water softener. The salt level was getting low. He'd better pick up a few bags of it. When he emerged from the basement, Nan was sitting at the table, bent over a piece of paper.

"I'll pick up some more pellets for your softener."

"Oh, good." She glanced up and smiled. "Thank you, dear. I want to make Brittany's favorite for dinner…" She stared at the wall.

"Is it still spaghetti?" He didn't want to talk about Brittany, but he didn't have it in him to hurt Nan's feelings.

"Yes." She frowned. "I think so."

"I'll pick up the ingredients. Don't worry."

Her shoulders relaxed and she handed him the list. "We'll be back in a few hours."

"Take Brittany with you. It'll be like old times."

Old times were best left in the past. He didn't say a word, just tipped his hat to her and walked out the back door. The faint sound of Noah's squeals in the distance made his heart pump faster. Was he all right? But unmistakable laughter assured him his boy was fine. Why it irritated him that his son was enjoying Brittany's company he didn't have the energy to analyze.

He strode through the snow to the barn. When he slid the door open, his gaze zoomed to Brittany's blond hair rippling down her back. Her smile could have illuminated the entire town. She stood to the side of the old tire swing.

He'd forgotten about the swing. Tired of its memories, he'd hauled it up to the hayloft years ago.

Sensations crashed into him.

It was their meeting place. The spot he'd rush to every day in the summer after his ranch chores were finished. The place he'd first kissed her. Even now, seeing her in front of it was doing something funny to his pulse.

Enough of that.

She must have gone up to the loft and let it drop down. Three sturdy ropes connected it to a beam above, and thick layers of straw cushioned the ground below it. The tire hovered horizontal to the ground so more than one person could ride on it at once.

The bottom of Noah's cowboy boots peeked through the tire, and his little arms grasped two of the ropes. As the swing went around, his shining, laughing face appeared. Mason couldn't help but smile, too. His innocence was precious.

"Can you believe the swing is still here?" Brittany's voice was laced with cordial undertones. Apparently she'd decided they should be civil. "The ropes are as strong as ever."

They were among the few things strong enough to survive these parts. He'd lost so many of his loved ones. First Ma, then Pops, then Mia… The weariness he'd been carrying for three years weighed on him.

"Noah, we'd better get moving."

She reached for the swing and stopped it. Then she helped Noah to his feet. He ran to Mason with his arms open. Mason caught him and hoisted him high in the air.

"I can fly!" Noah held his arms out.

Man, he loved this kid. He set Noah back down and turned to leave.

"Mason?"

He stopped, looking back.

"Nan's really going downhill, isn't she?"

Yeah, and if you cared, you'd be here more often. Brittany's rigid posture and the fear in her eyes kept the thoughts in his head, though.

"She's eighty-six." He wanted to say more but didn't.

"And you've been getting her groceries every week?" He nodded.

"For how long?" She looked vulnerable standing there.

"At least a year. Could be two, I guess. Why?" He cast a glance at Noah, who'd stopped in the corner to scoop kibble into the dishes. The barn cats were already stretching and heading over there.

"I… I didn't realize."

"Maybe if you visited more often, you would have known." He winced at his gruff tone and the harsh words. The dig, while true, pricked him with shame. He'd been studying the Bible more, thanks to Gabby and Eden and their Tuesday meetings, and one of the concepts they were all working on was choosing not to be bitter.

It was hard.

"How bad is she?" Brittany stepped forward, seemingly unmoved by his rudeness.

"Nothing I can't handle. If you'll excuse me." He pivoted, called to Noah and petted one of the cats before picking the boy up and marching straight outside.

He'd been taking care of Nan for a long time. Brittany didn't need to worry about it. He'd take care of the elderly woman until the day she died. She was as close to family as he had. Without her, he and Noah would still have the Pages, but it wasn't the same. Not for him, anyway.

Lately he'd been feeling like it was him against the world.

He thought of Ryder coming out this afternoon. For the first time since finding out he had a twin, Mason started to embrace the idea of having a brother.

"Do you need any clothes?" An hour later, Brittany sat on the living room floor folding the worn pants and shirts she'd taken out of the dryer. From the looks of it, Nan hadn't been clothes shopping in years. She pulled another sweatshirt out of the basket. In fact, a lot of things Brittany had assumed about Nan were questionable, like her ability to live independently out here on her own.

Before arriving, she'd assumed her grandmother was fine, still able to drive and shop for herself, and she'd assumed incorrectly. Nan was not fine. And Mason could claim he'd handle it, but Nan was her responsibility. Not his.

As for Mason's parting shot at her...

She sighed. He was right. She'd neglected Nan. Could her grandmother live by herself much longer?

"Did you say something?" Nan looked up from where

she sat in the recliner. A game show blared from the television.

"Why don't I take you shopping? I'd like to get you a new outfit." She pasted on her brightest smile and stacked another shirt on the pile.

"I've got a closet full of clothes, honey."

A closet full of outdated clothes that were too big. Maybe she could persuade Nan to go into Rendezvous and do a little shopping during the week. But did the small town even have a clothing store? She could always order a few items online.

After folding the final item, she rose and checked the time. It had been over an hour since Mason had left. Noah was the definition of adorable. He looked like his daddy. And that was a good thing.

Mason had grown more handsome since she'd last seen him. Broad shoulders, slim hips, muscular arms—he was all cowboy. His dark blond hair and caramel-brown eyes had always made her look twice at him. And the way her skin prickled with awareness when he'd been in the room earlier proved she wasn't immune to the man.

But now he wore an air of resignation, and every word he said had a bite to it.

He'd changed.

Grown harder. Gruffer.

Losing his wife must have been devastating.

As Nan's breathing settled to a soft snore, Brittany went to the kitchen to prep the fridge. It was stuffed with leftovers and rotting produce. *Gross.* She pulled out a trash bag and tossed the moldy and wilting food, then ran a soapy cloth over the fridge's shelves. Much better. The two cupboards where Nan kept her dry goods were in decent order.

The sound of a vehicle approaching alerted her Mason

was back. She debated her next move. Hide in her bedroom so he couldn't hurt her with accusations she already felt bad about? Or stay here and take his barbs straight on?

She deserved them. She'd failed Nan.

All the summers with her grandmother stood in her memories like happy greeting cards ready to be picked up and opened whenever she needed cheering. She loved Nan, and although she hadn't been able to spend much time with her in years, she wasn't going to let her down now. Not with her health declining.

Brittany opened the front door. Mason held brown paper bags in each hand, and Noah lugged a plastic bag as if it weighed a hundred pounds.

"How much more is there?" she asked.

"Another bag and the pellets for the water softener. I've got it."

"I'll put these away." She took one of the paper bags from him, and her hand brushed his. Awareness zipped through her, and a lump formed in her throat. This man—this stranger—had been her best friend most of her life. And now they couldn't even have a civil conversation.

His cheeks grew pink and he hustled back outside.

"Where does this go, Miss Bwittany?" Noah let his bag drop and wiped his forehead as if he was exhausted.

"What's in it?" She willed her emotions back into place and gave the boy what she hoped would pass for a smile.

"Toiwet paper." His lisp was so cute.

"Hmm…" She tapped her finger to her chin. "Where should we put the toilet paper?"

"The bathroom?" He took one of the handles and dragged the bag down the hallway as she set the milk and cream in the fridge. He ran back to her and peeked into the bags. "Can I help?"

"Sure." She pointed to the crackers and cookies. "Why don't you set these in the cupboard over there?"

He grabbed the cookies, threw open the cabinet door, tossed the package on top of canned vegetables and repeated the process with the crackers. Then he made a production out of wiping his hands. "Now what?"

Mason walked between them with two large bags of salt pellets on his shoulder.

Noah followed him to the basement door, then ran back to Brittany. "I don't like it down there."

She bent down to Noah's eye level. "I don't, either. It's dark and creepy."

"Yeah. Cweepy." He nodded, his expression a mixture of fear and excitement.

"Are you getting ready for Christmas?" She folded the paper bags.

"Yes! I'm getting presents! And Daddy's taking me to Christmas Fest!"

"He is?" She motioned for him to follow her to the table. "What's Christmas Fest?"

"Cookies and reindeer and an ice rink!" He climbed onto a chair on his knees.

"Well, that sounds like fun. I might have to check it out."

Mason's boots stomped up the steps. He looked at Noah. "Ready to go, buckaroo?"

"I wanna stay."

"We need to get our own groceries home."

Noah yawned, and Mason helped him put his coat on, then scooped him into his arms.

"Thank you." Brittany held the door open for them.

"Tell Nan I'll be over on Monday afternoon."

She blinked. "How often do you stop by?"

"Every day but Sunday. I'd take her to church, too, but Lois Dern insists on picking her up."

For once there wasn't any animosity in his gaze. Just the truth. And the truth hurt. He'd been taking care of Nan all this time, and Brittany hadn't even known Nan had needed help.

"I see." Her voice sounded as small as she felt.

He arched his eyebrows but didn't say a word. Then he carried Noah, who waved at her, down the steps to his truck.

She did see. And she didn't like the picture.

Mason had taken over Nan's care. His disdain for Brittany came through loud and clear.

Like most guys in her life, he'd decided she was all about herself.

Maybe she was.

They never seemed to understand that she had almost no free time and hadn't in years. Working multiple jobs and scraping pennies to have her own studio might be selfish, but it didn't make her a terrible person.

It looked like more changes to her life would need to be made. Nan was too important for Brittany to just leave her here without knowing she'd be safe. Mason might check on her in the afternoon, but what if Nan fell in the middle of the night? Got sick? Stopped paying her bills? Or grew more forgetful?

Was it time to look into assisted living?

Or…she supposed she could move Nan to California to live with her. Her head hurt at the thought. The logistics of it overwhelmed her.

She had time—a couple weeks—to figure out Nan's care.

What would be best for her grandmother?

Chapter Three

One question had been gnawing at him since finding Ryder on his porch last night. Which of them had been born first?

Mason strode beside Ryder down the path to the stables. Thankfully, Eden had offered to watch Noah for him. He'd briefly filled her in on the situation when he dropped Noah off after putting away the groceries. Eden, Mia's younger sister by three years, still lived with his in-laws. Bill and Joanna had gone Christmas shopping, allowing Mason to avoid having the *twin* conversation with them. They wouldn't be put off for long, however.

"Okay, now that you're here," Mason said, "I have a burning question."

"Shoot."

"When were you born? Which one of us is older?"

Ryder barked out a laugh. "I've been wondering the same thing. One of us is the big brother, and one is the baby. It's time we found out."

"My birth certificate says I was born at 5:43 a.m."

Ryder grimaced. "Mine says 5:54 a.m."

"I guess that means you're my little brother." Mason slapped him on the back. "By eleven minutes."

"And I guess it means you'll be rubbing it in forever."

"I guess it does." It didn't seem quite as bizarre to think of the man beside him as his brother anymore. He hitched his chin toward the stables. "You sure you want to ride?"

"I'd love to. I miss it," Ryder said. "I grew up on a sheep ranch in southern Montana."

"Sheep, huh?" Resentment between sheep ranchers and cattle ranchers had been simmering since the West had been settled. Both fought for grazing land, and both begrudged each other for it. Pops had never had a good thing to say about sheep ranchers.

He took a closer look at Ryder. His clothes were typical Western wear, but they were high quality, as were his expensive boots and hat. "You aren't still ranching?"

"No." He matched Mason's strides under the brilliant blue sky. "My grandparents got out of it when I was eleven. We moved closer to the city because Granddad needed medical care. Cancer took him a few years later."

Cancer. How he hated the disease that had stolen Mia from him. "Pops inherited this land along with the cow–calf operation and passed it down to me. Are you still living in Montana?"

"No. Moved out to California for college. I'm in the Los Angeles area. For now."

They reached the stables and Mason slid open the door. Dim light and floating dust motes greeted them as he led the way to the tack room. After hauling gear out, they saddled two quarter horses.

"Feels good to be out in the wide open again. It's been a long time." Ryder patted the neck of Rookie, one of Mason's favorite horses, as they rode toward the frozen-over creek. "I was torn about coming over, but this makes it worth it."

"Yeah, I'm sorry about last night." Mason hadn't put much thought into how Ryder might be handling having a twin. When had he gotten so self-absorbed? "It was a shock."

"For me, too. Finding out about you…well… Life has been chaotic lately." Ryder shrugged and nudged Rookie forward. Mason, riding Bolt, fell in beside him. "I'm glad you called this morning."

Mason was, too. And he knew all about chaos. Change had never been easy for him, and the past couple of years had been downright terrible. Noah had been the only thing worth waking up for besides the ranch. Mason would keep it running, even if it got to the point where he had to thin the herd further or let go of his extra ranch hands. He'd give this land to Noah someday.

"What do you do in LA?"

"I'm a CPA, and I do financial planning, as well." Ryder glanced around, taking in the hills. "Sometimes I miss this—outdoor living. My girls would love it out here."

"Twins, right? How old did you say they were?"

"Three and a half."

"Huh." That was a weird coincidence. "Noah is, too. When's their birthday?"

"March 24."

"Whoa-ho-ho." Mason shifted in his saddle as Ryder slowed Rookie. "That's Noah's birthday."

His eyes widened. "You mean they were born on the same day?"

"Just like we were." It seemed impossible. Yet he looked at his spitting image riding next to him and realized it *was* possible. Anything was, really. Suddenly, Mason wanted to know everything about this man. "I had appendicitis in the third grade."

"Me, too. January. Right after Christmas. I was glad to miss school."

"Same here!" A sense of wonder swirled in his mind. The man who looked just like him shared more than his appearance. They'd had kids on the same date, illnesses at the same time. "We shared a womb."

Ryder's mouth opened. He closed it without saying a word. Then he said, "I guess we did."

"Earlier someone stopped me at the grocery store and asked me if I ever sensed I had a twin. I can't say I did. Did you?" Actually, several people had stopped him earlier, and he'd practically sprinted out of there. Part of him was surprised he hadn't seen a line of cars in his drive when he got home.

"No, I had no idea I had a twin."

For the next thirty minutes, they rode along the creek and grilled each other about their childhoods. Laughter flowed freely, and more than once Mason caught Ryder inspecting him as if he couldn't quite believe his eyes. Neither volunteered information about the mothers of their children, though. He rarely talked about Mia outside of his Tuesday night meetings with Gabby and Eden, and Ryder had mentioned a divorce, so it must be a sore subject.

"Why'd they do it? Why keep us apart?" As they headed back to the stables, Mason hoped Ryder had more insight than he did. The deception bothered him. His memories of Ma and Pops didn't mesh with the reality saddled up next to him.

How could they have kept a brother from him? And why?

Ryder stared off into the distance. "I keep asking myself the same thing. I wish I knew. I can't ask my grandparents. They're long gone. I haven't been back to my hometown since I was a kid."

"Someone must have known. How did we just now learn about each other? If anyone around here knew, I'd have found out long ago. Secrets are spilled on a regular basis in these parts."

Ryder's jaw shifted. "To be frank with you, I haven't asked myself too many questions because I know I won't like the answers. It was enough to come out here and meet you."

A gust of wind chilled Mason.

"I'm leaving tomorrow." Ryder glanced his way. "I know this is sudden, but I'd like to come back. I have the last two weeks of December off. Would it bother you if I brought my girls out here to meet you?"

He usually resisted last-minute plans, but he wanted to meet his nieces.

I have nieces. With all the information he'd been trying to process, it hadn't sunk in that he was an uncle. The thought warmed his heart.

"I'd like that. Stay here with the girls. And why don't you have supper with me and Noah tonight? I gave him the condensed version of you earlier. Be prepared for a lot of questions."

"Okay."

"I know I wasn't the welcome wagon yesterday, but… having a brother is pretty cool."

"Maybe there's a simple explanation for why we never knew about each other." Ryder's smile lit his eyes. "I guess we have Brittany to thank for finding each other."

"I guess we do," he said quietly. Ryder had a point. As much as Mason wanted to leave the past in the past, maybe he should stop in at Nan's tomorrow before Brittany left and thank her for introducing them.

It wouldn't mean anything had changed. It was simply the right thing to do.

But the image of her smiling face as she pushed Noah on the tire swing earlier made him pause. Maybe he should leave well enough alone. It was safer to hang on to a decade-old grudge than to let Brittany's sunshine into his life again.

After Mia's death, he'd made a promise to himself. There could be no one else. He'd already had the best.

I'll never let you go, Mia.

Brittany tapped her pen against the blank spiral notebook page. Fifteen minutes of brainstorming had yielded no results.

Nan had lived in this house ever since she'd gotten married at eighteen. After two days here, Brittany wasn't sure Nan would be able to live on her own for much longer.

But what could she do about it?

At meals, Nan picked at her food. She most likely skipped eating altogether when left to her own devices. Her bony frame could use more nourishment.

Also, from the smell of it, Nan wasn't bathing regularly. She used to shower first thing in the morning. When Brittany suggested she take a shower, Nan claimed she'd washed up yesterday, which was not true. How long had it been since she'd shampooed her hair?

Other things nagged at her, as well. The house was tidy, but dust covered every surface, and the floors hadn't seen a mop in a long time. Yesterday afternoon, Brittany had scrubbed the house, but how long would it last?

She stretched her arms over her head. Nan was resting in her room. The Sunday service had tuckered her out.

After church, Gretchen Sable, a sweet older lady who

was friends with Nan, had pulled Brittany aside, given her a paper with her number on it, patted her hand and told her to call her anytime.

At least the church was the same as it had been a decade ago. Sure, the old blue carpet had been replaced, but familiar worship songs had filled the air and the message of grace had not fallen on deaf ears. It reminded Brittany of her church back home.

That was another thing to thank her grandmother for—Nan was the one who'd told her about Jesus and encouraged her to pray.

The last time she'd attended a Sunday service here with Nan, she'd been eighteen and full of excitement about the future. Now? She hadn't fulfilled her dreams. They'd never included scrimping to pay bills, teaching only a handful of classes and renting a run-down matchbox of an apartment.

Success had eluded her in every area.

The sharp pang of discouragement tore through her chest. Had her entire adult life been a waste? Had she made the wrong choices?

Her mother certainly thought so and wasn't afraid to say it. As for Brittany's father, she had his last name, but he had never been part of her life. Now that Mom was busy traveling as a corporate consultant, Brittany rarely talked to her, either. It wasn't as if she cared what the woman thought anymore. God saw Brittany's heart and didn't judge her by her lack of progress. So why was she judging herself so harshly?

She tossed down the pen and massaged her temples. She was supposed to be coming up with solutions for Nan's care, not wallowing in some strange what-had-she-done-with-her-life crisis.

The sound of a vehicle coming up the drive broke her

concentration. She peeked out the window and recognized Mason's truck. Why was he here? Whatever the reason, her pulse sped at the thought of seeing him again.

She put her coat on and shoved her feet into her boots to meet him on the porch. The air was crisp and the frozen countryside beautiful. He strode up tall, sure of himself. The cowboy boots, hat and jeans fit him like a glove. Her stomach did a pirouette. She looked for signs of Noah, but the boy wasn't with him. Too bad. He was a cutie.

His eyes weren't as hard and judgmental today. A girl could get lost in those depths.

"What are you doing here?" she asked.

"I wanted to talk to you for a minute."

"I'd ask you inside, but Nan is sleeping right now." She tucked her hair behind her ear. "Actually, I wanted to speak with you, too."

"If this is about what happened way back when…" His expression grew wary.

"No." She waved him off. "It's been a long time. We've both moved on with our lives." She fought for a chipper tone. Talking to Mason used to be easy—from the day she'd met him until the day she'd left. This awkwardness felt wrong—understandable, but wrong. "I wanted to talk to you about Nan. About how she's doing."

He widened his stance, crossing his arms over his chest. Formidable.

"I don't like it when you tower over me. I know it's cold, but let's sit."

His left eyebrow cocked skyward, but he followed her to the rocking chairs on the covered porch.

She sat in one and waited while he settled into the other. She was all too aware his knee was only inches from hers. "Nan isn't the same."

"The same? What do you mean?"

She'd never been good at this—being blunt. Never quite knew how to approach a subject without offending someone. And it tended to result in her rambling.

"She's gotten thin. Just this morning I caught her hiking up the elastic on her black church pants, and let me tell you, they still drooped. And her hair really concerns me. I mean, how many days does she go without showering? It's so unlike her." Without thinking, she rose to her feet and stretched to her tiptoes before sitting down again.

"I hadn't noticed."

How could he *not* have noticed? She turned to face him. "She sleeps more. Drifts in and out all day long. You know how she used to be. Capable. Self-sufficient. She drove everywhere, baked up a storm, made jam, quilted. This house was always spotless, and she'd sit in her rocker with a book most afternoons, and she'd have this peaceful, happy expression on her face. I loved that." Her heart simultaneously warmed and pinched thinking about it. She hugged herself. "But now? She's forgetful. Confused. And frail."

He leaned back, crossing an ankle over his knee. "She's getting up there in age. What did you expect?"

What did she expect? If she were being honest with herself, she hadn't wanted to face the thought of Nan being anything other than the strong, kind woman who'd taught her how to pray and to be comfortable in her own skin. It had been delusional on her part to expect Nan to still be a powerhouse at eighty-six.

"I don't know." Her head dropped. "I just don't know."

He didn't say anything. Simply sat there, quiet and still.

She'd always struggled with stillness. Even now, her arms and legs longed to move, explore the space and, to some extent, help her come to terms with what she was feeling. A series of pique turns down the length of the porch enticed her. But she kept her feet rooted in place.

"You check on her most days and get her groceries." She shivered. It was really cold out here.

"Yep."

"She doesn't seem fit to drive anymore."

"I don't think she is. Lois Dern takes her to the beauty parlor every other week, so she is getting her hair washed, and one of the other church ladies, Gretchen Sable, I think, takes her to the doctor if she needs to go."

Just what she'd suspected—Nan was trapped in this house, far away from help. It couldn't be safe for her.

"I think her days living alone are numbered." Brittany sighed.

"She's fine." His expression hardened. "I won't let anything happen to her."

"You?"

"Yeah, me." His eyes narrowed. "I've taken care of her this long. I'll take care of her for good."

"She's my grandmother."

"Could have fooled me."

"Wow. Really?" She raised her chin and glared at him. "Oh, that's right, you know everything there is to know about me, and I must still be the selfish liar who left town ten years ago. I couldn't possibly care about anyone but myself, right?"

"If the shoe fits." His face grew red, but he continued to sit there, ankle resting without even a twitch on his knee. How could he be so calm?

"Forget it." She got up, spun away from him and looked out over the porch rail. "Go back to your ranch. I'll take care of Nan."

"And how are you going to do that, California?"

Did he really just call her California? Her temper didn't

flair often, but when it did, things could get ugly, and she felt the storm brewing inside her. *Lord, help me stay calm. Grant me patience.*

She whirled and caught her breath. He'd moved to stand behind her, and his nearness, his height slammed her with memories. She knew exactly how those hands would feel at her waist. The precise height she'd need to rise up to wrap her arms around his neck and...

She couldn't get mushy. It had taken her years to get over him. One touch and all could be lost.

"Why don't you get it all out right now, Mason? Say all the miserable things you've been thinking about me. Go on. I can take it."

His jaw shifted but he kept his mouth shut.

She was tired of carrying around the shame about him and their past. She'd been a stupid teenager. And it had cost her dearly.

"I'm sorry for hurting you back then." She stood tall. "I should have broken up with Parker before I came here that summer. He and I weren't right for each other. I'd known it for months. I thought with me being away, he'd figure it out, too." Saying the truth out loud deflated the bravado she'd had moments ago. "It doesn't matter—I should have told you about him. I should have done a lot of things differently that summer."

"Yes, you should have." His voice was hard.

"I know." And she did. But even if she had... "It wouldn't have changed the ending, though. I couldn't have stayed here. You and I both know it."

His throat worked as he swallowed. He took his time mulling it over. Then he met her eyes, and she relaxed. Those were the eyes she remembered. The warm, caring man she used to know was still in there somewhere.

"I reckon you're right." The words were soft, sincere and they slammed into her heart. "I've missed you, Brit."

She'd missed him, too. More than he would ever know.

"I only came around today to thank you for introducing me to Ryder."

"You're welcome." She looked at this rugged man and saw beneath the tough exterior to the hurts inside. He'd lost too much in his life. How she'd wanted to be there for him when his grandparents died, and then Mia... But she wouldn't have been welcome. "You always wanted a brother. I couldn't deny you that."

"Thank you." He nodded. "And don't worry about Nan. She's not sick. She'll be fine. We look out for our own in Rendezvous."

"I know you do. I appreciate all you've done for her. But I can't handle worrying about her every day. And I will worry. I think it's time I consider moving Nan to California with me."

"What?" His mind reeled. One minute he was flinging out ugly words he'd never meant to say, the next she was apologizing for that summer and hitting him with the truth like a slap to the face. He believed she regretted her actions that summer, and deep down he knew she was right about not being able to stay. But this—taking Nan from him—was going too far. "No, it's not necessary. California? Really, Brittany? Can't you think about anyone but yourself?"

"Now who's the one being selfish?" She gave him a cool glare. "I'm thinking about Nan. What if she falls and no one finds her for hours?"

"We'll get her one of those emergency buttons." Even as the words left his mouth, he wondered if Brittany was right. Was he being selfish for wanting to keep Nan right where she was?

"She's barely keeping up with basic hygiene. I feel like she's living on yogurt and cheese crackers. The house is dirty. And so is she. She's confused."

"I'll hire someone to help out with the cleaning once a week. We can pick up frozen dinners for her. All she'll have to do is pop them in the microwave." Easy solutions. No need for her to move Nan to another state.

"But will she?"

"Yes." But he wasn't so sure she actually would. He tried to imagine how Nan must appear in Brittany's eyes, and he admitted, the picture wasn't great.

"How long can this last? Six months? A year? I have to think long-term." She covered her face with her hands and wiped her cheeks. She rose on her tippy-toes again, a movement he knew meant she was conflicted.

For the first time, he allowed himself to really see Brittany. Fine lines creased around her eyes and between her eyebrows. Her life might not have been as happy-go-lucky as he'd imagined.

That didn't change things. He wasn't letting her rip Nan away from here.

"Nan should have a say in it, too." And so should he.

"I know." She bit the corner of her lip, worry running through those pretty blue eyes.

"Look, I know you have a busy life in California," he said as gently as possible. "I've been watching out for Nan a long time. She's like a grandmother to me."

"But she's my grandma."

That point stung a bit. Technically, Nan was Brittany's grandmother, but he'd spent enough time with her to lay claim to the title, too, hadn't he?

"And I don't appreciate your tone when you talk about

my busy life in California. You don't know anything about my life. And it *is* busy, just not in the frivolous way you're implying. If I move Nan in with me, I'll be able to take care of her."

"How are you going to do that? You'll have to drag her out of this house kicking and screaming. She's lived here for over sixty years. I'm sure it will do wonders for her health being stuck in the smog and surrounded by people all the time."

"Look, I didn't say I was moving her out there for sure. I merely said I was considering it."

"Will you even be around to take care of her?" In his mind he'd always pictured Brittany laughing and living a social life surrounded by adoring friends. Honestly, the thought made him jealous. His life had been full of responsibility since he was a young boy.

"What do you think I do? I'm not some party girl flying around. I teach children and teens dance lessons at night and work part-time at a diner on weekends. During the day, I pick up side jobs doing data entry from home. So, to answer your question, no, I won't always be around to take care of her. But you aren't, either, so I don't think you can talk."

She worked three jobs? A diner? Data entry? It wasn't meshing with his idea of her at all. "Why so many jobs?"

"Because being a dance teacher doesn't pay the big bucks, I've been trying to pay off my student loans, Santa Ana is expensive and I want to open my own dance studio."

"Oh." Shame didn't feel very good. For years he'd wanted to tell her off, to see her miserable, and all the while, he'd believed she was living the fabulous life. He'd been wrong, and gloating didn't appeal even the tiniest bit.

For the first time in a decade, he wouldn't mind if Brittany was happy.

"If it's tough making ends meet, how will you be able to take care of Nan, too?"

Her shoulders drooped. "I don't know. I'll find a way."

"Why don't you take some time to think about it?" Maybe if she went back to California without Nan, she'd forget about moving her. Or, at the very least, it wouldn't feel as urgent. Then he'd still be able to drop by here every afternoon and nothing would change.

He was sick of changes that meant losing the ones he loved.

"I can do that." She stared out at the distance, then nodded. "I'm not going back to California until after Christmas."

His mind blanked. She was staying until after Christmas? Two whole weeks?

"I thought you were flying back with Ryder."

"No, I wanted to spend Christmas with Nan." She met his eyes. "I can check out assisted-living facilities and look into having someone come here a few days a week. If neither of those seem like good options, I'll have to consider moving her to California with me."

"I want to have some say in Nan's future, too." He didn't care if he wasn't blood related.

"Fair enough." Her half-hearted smile didn't light her eyes. "I owe you that. Thanks for everything you've done for Nan. I… I can't thank you enough." She reached over and covered his hand with hers.

Her touch instantly transported him back to when she was his. Back to when life seemed full of possibility, not trouble and death.

He slipped his hand out from under hers.

"You gave me my brother. Let's call it even. I've got

to pick up Noah." He tipped his hat to her. "I'll stop by tomorrow afternoon."

He hurried back to his truck. Once inside, he exhaled loudly. Brittany's touch, her presence had made him do and say things he hadn't planned. As he drove away, he gripped the steering wheel. Between Ryder and her, his life felt unrecognizable.

He frowned. For the first time in three years, he'd completely forgotten about Mia. In fact, he hadn't thought about her in hours.

His throat tightened and his vision blurred.

He couldn't forget her. Wouldn't forget her.

He would not let ocean-blue eyes erase her memory. Mia was the love of his life, and Brittany being in town for two weeks wouldn't change it.

Nothing would.

Chapter Four

"What about this sweater?" Brittany held up a cardigan at Sissy's Bargain Clothes in downtown Rendezvous. The cream-colored sweater was a size medium. Nan had been wearing a large for years, but the way her clothes hung on her now, Brittany assumed a medium was the right size.

"It would look nice on you." Nan clutched her purse and stood stiffly.

"No, Nan, I meant for you." Christmas music played in the background, and gold tinsel garland was draped above them. None of it was getting her in the Christmas spirit, though. After yesterday's revealing chat with Mason, she was more confused than ever. Did he still hate her or had he meant it when he said he missed her? Either way, he thought she was a lousy granddaughter.

That made two of them.

"Why don't you try it on?" Brittany pasted on a bright smile, but she felt it sliding away at Nan's blank expression. *Stay cool, Brit.* She gamely held the garment up to her grandmother. Would the sleeves be long enough?

"Oh, no. I'll just watch you shop."

The entire morning had been a struggle. From trying to convince Nan to shower—Brittany had won that battle—

to searching for Nan's car keys—they were on the book-shelf, behind a shepherdess figurine—she'd been all too aware that Nan's pace and hers were worlds apart.

Even getting to town had been difficult. The old Ford truck in the detached garage had coughed back to life after several wheezing attempts at starting it. At least none of the tires had been flat. From the layers of dust on the hood, dash and seats, she guessed it had been many months since Nan had driven it anywhere.

It was a good thing Nan wasn't driving, but her home-bound state weighed on Brittany. She must be very lonely.

"I'll grab a few pairs of pants and another sweater, and you can try them all on at once." She kept her tone cheery as she rounded up three pairs of the elastic-band pants Nan favored, another sweater and two sweatshirts. "The dressing rooms are back here."

Brittany carried the clothes to the doors decorated with Christmas wreaths along the wall. Nan shuffled behind her.

"Here you go." She hung up the clothes on the hooks provided. "I'll be right out here. Let me know when you have them on. You can model them for me."

Nan's forehead furrowed as she slunk into the room. Brittany sighed. Was she pushing her too hard? Well, what was the alternative? The woman needed new clothes.

A minute ticked by. Then two. She strained to hear movement from inside the dressing room. Finally, she knocked.

"Nan? How's it going in there?"

The door opened and there stood Nan, still in her win-ter coat with the clothes pristinely hanging up as if they hadn't been touched.

"Did you try them on?"

"No." She glanced back at the hooks.

"Why not?"

"I don't know." Nan looked lost. "I suppose I forgot."

Her heart squeezed. She'd only been in there for a few minutes! How could she have forgotten? Brittany put her arm around Nan's slim shoulders. "It's okay. Let's go ahead and buy them. I think they'll all fit. If not, we can return them."

Brittany collected all the clothes and made her way to the checkout. She waited for the chatty clerk to ring up everything and fold them into neat bags. After she paid, she turned around, expecting to see Nan behind her.

But she was gone.

Brittany scanned the store, saw no sign of her grandmother and jogged outside. Looking left then right down Centennial Street, the main drag in Rendezvous where most of the shops and businesses were located, she tried to catch a glimpse of her. Maybe she'd gone back to the truck. Brittany stretched her neck to see the truck parked down the block, but it was empty.

Don't panic.

Where would Nan go? The sun was shining, the temperature brisk. Too cold to be outside for long. She scanned the area. Christmas garlands, bows and twinkle lights bedecked the storefronts. Cattle Drive Coffee was across the street. A beauty shop was next door. A Western store, bakery and insurance office filled out this side of the block.

She'd have to check each one. Quickly, she peeked inside the first set of front windows. Up ahead, the door to the bakery opened, and Nan walked out with a small bag. Relief weakened her knees, but she raced up the sidewalk. "Nan, over here!"

"I was hungry for fritters." She held the bag up, a big smile on her face.

"Why didn't you wait? I would have come with you." She

tucked Nan's arm in hers and tried to will away the fear in her throat. "Next time, let me know you're leaving, okay?"

"What time is it?" Nan frowned. "I need to get home. Mason will be coming."

"He won't be there until later." Brittany took out her phone and showed her the time. "Let's get lunch."

Nan patted her arm. "I'd like that. Mason loves Roscoe's chocolate chip cookies. Can we pick him up a few before we leave?"

And just like that, Nan seemed herself again. Brittany breathed a sigh of relief. Roscoe's Diner was a staple in Rendezvous. She steered Nan in its direction.

Maybe Mason's daily check-ins were grounding her grandmother more than Brittany had considered. She might not love that he was demanding to have a say in Nan's future, but like it or not, he deserved it. He'd been taking care of her for this long.

A sharp pain of guilt stabbed her conscience, but she refused to wallow in it. She'd neglected her grandmother, but she wouldn't anymore. Nan's health and happiness were too important. *Thank You, God, for Mason's kindness to Nan.*

As they crossed the street, she mentally made a list. She needed to make a doctor's appointment to find out exactly what was wrong with Nan. Was her forgetfulness a normal sign of aging? Or was it something worse, like dementia or Alzheimer's?

Every day with her grandmother brought new questions. Someone had to have answers.

Maybe Nan's friends, Gretchen and Lois, could give her some insight, too.

Mason stirred the pot of beans on the stove later that evening. The hot dogs were sizzling on his indoor grill pan. "Noah, it's time to eat!"

There was a knock on the front door. His palms grew sweaty. He'd invited his in-laws over. The time had come to have the twin talk.

"I'll get it, Daddy!" Little footsteps pounded from the living room where a cartoon played on the television.

"No, Noah, let me." With long strides, he reached the foyer at the same time as Noah. "What did I tell you about opening the door?"

"Not s'posed to." He hung his head. "Could be a stranger."

"Right." He peeked out the window at the top of the door. His in-laws had arrived early.

"Grandpa!" Noah launched his body toward Bill.

"Hey, Spurs, didn't I just see you?" Bill's face was full of affection as he lifted Noah in his arms. He was short, barrel-chested and physically tough, even though he'd turned sixty-five last month.

"Doesn't Grandma get a hug?" Joanna's love for her grandson was written all over her face. At sixty-one, she had shoulder-length dark brown hair, kind gray eyes and wrinkles at the corners of her eyes and mouth. Mia would have looked just like her if she'd grown old.

Mason expected the familiar ache at the thought, but it didn't come. *Huh.*

Noah wriggled in Bill's arms and held out his hands to Joanna, who laughed and kissed his cheek.

"Thanks for coming over." Mason helped Joanna with her coat. "I was just putting supper on the table. Have you eaten?"

"Yes, but we'll sit with you if you don't mind."

"Sit next to me, Grandpa!"

Bill carried Noah to the kitchen, with Mason and Joanna trailing behind.

Mason took the hot dogs off the grill and served a

plate of food to Noah. He'd eat later. His appetite wasn't great at the moment.

"It's about time we discussed your, ah, twin. People are asking us questions." Bill leaned forward with his hands clasped and forearms resting on the table.

"I'm sure. Sorry about that."

"Yeah, well, you could have filled us in sooner," Bill said.

Fair enough. Mason could have…but he hadn't wanted to. Was it too much to ask to work through a major shock in private for a few days?

Joanna tried to ease the tension. "What's he like, Mason?"

"Uncle Ryder looks just like Daddy, Grandma!" Ketchup dribbled down his chin. "He ate supper with us and everything. Daddy, do you think 'nother uncle's out there?"

Another uncle? Mason tried to figure out what he meant.

"I'm sure your uncle Ryder is the only one you haven't met." Joanna smiled, scrunching her nose at Noah.

"Are you sure?" Noah asked.

Mason hadn't considered the possibility there could be other siblings he didn't know about. What if they'd been part of triplets? Quadruplets? He squashed the thought. Both sets of grandparents would have taken *all* the babies if there were more than two. That was one thing he could be certain of.

"Tell us what you know." Bill seemed to stare straight into his soul.

Mason squirmed. *God, I feel like I'm stepping on eggshells here. I need Your help. I'm tired of disappointing this man, and something tells me what I'm about to say will disappoint him, too.*

"There's not much to tell. Friday night he showed up on my doorstep."

"No warning? Out of the blue?" Joanna's eyes grew wide. "How did he find out you existed? And where did he get your address?"

"An old friend of mine ran into him in California. Thought he was me."

"An old friend, huh?" Bill sat up straighter. "Babs mentioned Ada's granddaughter happens to be in town."

"Who's Ada, Grandpa?" Noah lifted a spoonful of beans to his mouth.

"That's Nan, honey." Joanna patted his head. "If memory serves me right, you and her granddaughter were close once upon a time, weren't you?" The only thing missing from this prosecution was a gavel.

"Yes, Brittany Green was the one who introduced Ryder and me." He flexed his hands. Bill and Joanna had lived in Rendezvous their entire lives. They knew everything and everyone. It wasn't a shock to hear they remembered him being close to Brittany. But he'd divided his life into pre-Mia and post-Mia, and Brittany had never fit into the post-Mia portion.

"Why didn't she call?" Joanna asked.

"She did. I didn't answer." Was he ever going to get to the meat of the story? Or were they going to be hung up on Brittany for the duration? "They showed up, we started piecing things together and we're trying to figure out how to move forward."

"The three of you?" Bill asked.

"No. Ryder and I."

Joanna fanned her face. "I can't believe none of us knew you were a twin. Your grandparents sure knew how to keep a secret."

"Yeah, tell me about it." Mason arched his eyebrows.

He'd taken for granted that no one had answers for him. But his in-laws might know something he didn't. "Ryder was raised by one set of grandparents. I was raised by the other. If you have any information to fill in the blanks, I'd love to hear it."

Joanna sat back in her chair. "I remember when John, your father, went away to college. Your grandfather expected him to come back and join him in ranching. But things grew strained between them the following summer. And then your grandparents didn't talk about him anymore. Everyone stopped asking. It was a sore subject."

"Was anyone close to Ma and Pops who might know more?"

"They've all passed on by now." Joanna shook her head sympathetically. "Well, except Ada. She's never been one to gossip, though."

"I guess I could ask her."

"I'm assuming no one around here knew you were twins," Joanna said. "Someone would have spilled it long ago. All we knew was that your folks eloped, were killed in a car crash right after you were born, and your grandparents brought home the baby—you—to raise."

"If you think of anything, even if it's minor, would you let me know?" Mason asked her.

"Of course." She gave him a tender smile. "Did your grandparents keep old albums or anything? I wonder if there would be something here that might give you a clue."

It wouldn't hurt to look.

"Ma left several boxes of documents and pictures up in the attic. I haven't had time to find them, but I'll bring them down tonight. Maybe I'll find something."

"And while you're up there, bring your Christmas decorations down." Bill gave him a hard stare. "Christmas is less than two weeks off."

"We can decorate for you again if you'd like." Joanna handed Noah a napkin. He'd eaten half his hot dog. Last year, Joanna and Bill had set up his Christmas tree and decorated it with candy canes and crafts Eden helped Noah make. The year before, he'd skipped decorating altogether. Noah climbed off his chair and took off running.

"Wait, Noah, you need to wipe your hands." Joanna rose, motioning for Mason to stay seated. "I'll get him cleaned up."

When she'd left, Bill leaned in closer. "I know you're working through some stuff, but Noah needs a nice Christmas. Don't deprive him of the fun of the season. He's only young once."

"He'll have a good Christmas." Nothing he did was ever good enough in Bill's eyes. Maybe he shouldn't have let them decorate last year.

"If you need help…"

"I don't."

"Are you sure about that? Your calf sales weren't what they should have been."

"Yeah, well, nothing is anymore, now is it?" Mason massaged his right temple. He'd asked Bill to help him prep the calves for the sale last month. He'd needed every hand he could get. But maybe it had been a mistake.

"I don't want you falling apart. You've got your boy to think about."

"Don't you think I know that?" He wanted to jump up and storm off, but he forced himself to look Bill in the eye. "I've got it under control."

"All right. I can see I'm not wanted." He stood and put his hands out in front of him. "I'll take your word for it you'll do Christmas up right for Noah. As for the ranch, you should have kept more replacement heifers. Your herd is thinning."

Mason bristled. He hadn't told Bill and Joanna about the enormous medical bills Mia had left behind. He hadn't told anyone. The last thing he needed was the entire town knowing his financial problems. And as for the heifers, yeah, he should have—would have—kept more but the bills kept pouring in and he'd had to sell more cattle than he'd wanted to.

Joanna returned holding Noah's hand. His face was squeaky-clean.

A knock came from the front door.

What now? Another brother?

He excused himself to go answer it.

Brittany stood on the doormat. His pulse quickened at the sight of her. Then he checked the rest of the porch. No one was with her. He sighed in relief. Ever since Noah mentioned more uncles, a part of him had worried...

"No other long-lost brothers of mine?" he asked.

"No, just the one." She flashed a grin. "Can I come in?"

"It's not—"

"I have to talk to you about Nan." She pushed past him into the foyer, leaving a trail of floral scent in her wake.

"We won't keep you." Joanna touched Mason's shoulder, and he almost jumped. Shifting, he saw Bill and Joanna getting into their coats. Noah scampered beside them.

"You don't have to go," Mason said, although he wanted them to leave.

"Miss Bwittany!" Noah ran up to her and gave her a hug. She laughed and hugged him back.

His father-in-law eyed him and Brittany like they were naughty teenagers.

"Bill, Joanna, do you remember Nan's granddaughter, Brittany?" Mason forced a pleasant tone.

"Nice to meet you." Joanna held out a hand.

"The pleasure's mine." Brittany shook it and turned to Bill. "Good to meet you, sir."

Bill nodded, then turned to Mason. "Don't forget. Christmas decorations."

"Bye, Grandpa! Bye, Grandma!" Noah jumped up and down.

They said their goodbyes and left. Before Mason could shut the door, he noticed Bill glance backward. He looked annoyed at Brittany.

Mason wasn't exactly thrilled to have her here, either. He wanted to eat his supper, read a few books to Noah, then find the boxes in the attic his grandmother had stored. Start piecing together his lost childhood. He needed answers.

And Bill was right. He needed to deal with Christmas—another thing he'd failed at lately. He wished his father-in-law would stop assuming the worst. He had every intention of giving Noah a wonderful Christmas. He just hadn't had much time.

Sighing, he waved toward the living room. "Come in."

Well, that was awkward. Brittany hadn't realized his in-laws were there, although she should have known someone was visiting since there was a truck parked out front.

She'd wanted to talk to Mason this afternoon when he'd stopped by to check on Nan, but he hadn't stayed long. Then, after he'd left, more questions had sprung up. So she'd driven over.

Maybe she should have called. Or texted.

If she was brutally honest with herself, she'd needed

to get out of the house for a few minutes. The slow pace compared to her go-go-go life in Santa Ana was getting to her, and Nan had fallen asleep on the couch right after supper, anyhow.

"Want to see the cards I made with Auntie Eden?" Noah tugged on her hand.

"Of course!" She aimed for the right amount of excitement.

"I'll get them." His little legs bounded up the staircase.

"I'll make it quick," she said to Mason. In a navy flannel shirt and jeans, he seemed more approachable than he had earlier. A ripple of awareness flashed over her skin. "Do you know anything about Nan's finances? Is she keeping up with them? And do you know how she pays her bills?"

"I'm not sure." He frowned. "Did you look in her checkbook?"

"No, I asked her if she had a system, and she gave me a vague answer. With the way she's slowing down, I was worried she might be forgetting other things, too." Brittany rubbed her chin. "But I'll ask to look at her checkbook. By the way, do you know who her doctor is?"

"I can't imagine she'd go to anyone other than Doctor Landson. He's been seeing her for years."

"Good." His eyes held warring emotions. Something was bothering him, but the warmth in them told her it wasn't her. In fact, the way he was staring brought butterflies of old to her tummy. "What's wrong?"

"Want to get a Christmas tree?" His voice was low.

She blinked. "Right now?"

"No." The corner of his mouth hooked upward. "Soon, though."

A Christmas tree? With him? Nan's house was devoid of Christmas decorations at the moment. Maybe she could get a tree for Nan, too. It would be nice to deck her house all out. She shrugged. "Sure."

Noah barreled down the steps with a fistful of construction paper. He took her hand and led her to the couch.

"Sit by me." Noah climbed onto the couch and patted the cushion next to him. Brittany glanced at Mason to see if she should make an excuse and leave, but the gleam in his eye told her it was okay to stay a minute. She sat next to the little boy.

"This one's for Aunt Gabby." He spread out a folded green paper with two stick figures—one big, one small. "It's her and Phoebe."

"Who's Phoebe?" Brittany admired the card.

"Aunt Gabby's baby. Auntie Eden babysits her, and I help."

"You're a good helper, aren't you?"

"I am." He puffed up his chest and lifted his chin. "Babies need lots of help. I tickle her tummy and she laughs. And sometimes I get to hold her bottle when she eats. I don't drink out of a bottle cuz I'm a big boy."

"You sure are. That's good of you to help with the baby."

"This one's for Grandma." He showed her a pink paper. It had blue handprints on it. "She likes pink. Those are my hands."

"They are? So big. And blue." She gave him a big smile. "You did a good job."

Noah popped his head up to look around. She did the same. Mason had disappeared. Noah leaned in and held a finger to his lips. "Shh...this one's for Daddy." He proudly held up a light gray paper. It had two stick figures with hats, one smaller than the other. They were holding hands. A female stick figure was at the side. "I asked Santa for a mommy."

"You did?" She leaned closer, enjoying his excitement, but inwardly cringing at his wish. He spent so much time with his babysitter, he probably wanted her to be his mommy.

"Uh-huh." He nodded, his eyes bright. "A nice one."

"The best kind." She winked at him. She wouldn't destroy his hopes. For all she knew, Mason could be dating someone in town. The thought didn't make her happy.

Light footsteps approached. Brittany stood up. "Thanks for showing me your pictures, Noah. I'd better get back to Nan's. Maybe I'll see you tomorrow."

"Bye!" He waved from the couch.

Mason escorted her to the front door.

"Were you serious about getting a Christmas tree?" She reached for the door handle. If he had a girlfriend in town, he wouldn't be asking Brittany to go with him, that was for sure.

Hesitation flitted through his eyes, but he nodded.

"I thought…maybe you'd want another girl to go with you."

His expression clouded. "No. Mia was it for me."

Why it hurt to hear him say that, she didn't know. Mason was like that—loyal to a fault. "Okay, let me know when."

"I've got a meeting tomorrow night, but what about Wednesday afternoon? I'll pick up Noah from Eden's, and the three of us can go together."

"I'd like to get one for Nan, too, if you don't mind."

"I don't mind."

"I…um…wanted to thank you. For all you've been doing for Nan." She opened the door a sliver. "I know with me there you don't need to check on her, but would you keep coming?"

"I plan on it. Why do you ask?"

"She's forgetful about a lot of things, but she always knows when you're due to stop by. I think you keep her grounded."

"I like visiting her." He put his hand on the edge of the door and opened it wider. His nearness crowded her senses. "I'll stop by tomorrow afternoon at the usual time."

"Thanks." She hurried outside. As she tromped across the hard ground, she clutched her coat to her body tightly.

She hadn't expected a truce. She also hadn't expected the attraction between them to flame back to life. At least she knew it was one-sided. He was still mourning his wife.

She'd suppressed her feelings for Mason for over a decade. Being back in Rendezvous was messing with her head—that was all. In no time at all, she'd return to California and to the goals that had eluded her for years.

Please let the bank call with good news.

If it didn't?

I can't go on like this—I need a win.

She got into the truck and peeked back at Mason's house. At least she seemed to be getting Mason's friendship back. Even if it was only for the holidays.

Chapter Five

Tuesday, after moving cattle to a new pasture and checking on the pregnant cows, Mason tore off his Carhartt jacket and jogged to the den where he'd set four boxes from the attic last night. He rarely went up there because everything was such a jumbled mess. But he'd found several boxes with old photos and documents, and he'd deemed these the most likely to hold answers. He'd made it through half a box last night before giving in to exhaustion.

With less than an hour before he had to pick up Noah, he set the alarm on his phone to get through as much as he could.

The piles he'd already sorted were stacked to the side. He folded his limbs into a sitting position on the floor and reached into the box. Photographs from the old days—what looked like the thirties and forties—appeared. While he enjoyed seeing his ancestors and images from the past, he didn't have time to linger. Quickly, he sorted through photographs, newspaper clippings and postcards.

Nothing.

After a quick sift through the remaining items in the box, he hauled over a different one. He lifted the lid and saw much of the same: old pictures—some in color this time—manuals, receipts, postcards and such. He prepared to put the lid back on it, but a picture caught his eye. A little boy who looked like Noah.

Mason studied the photo and flipped it over. Scrawled on the back was *John—4 years old*.

His dad. Blond, big grin, skinny, in jeans and a white T-shirt. Mason hadn't realized Noah resembled his father so much.

He hadn't looked at a photo album since Ma and Pops died. Prior to that, it had been years since he'd gone down memory lane. But seeing his dad looking so much like Noah made him wonder if he resembled them, too.

He stood and set the picture of his dad on the fireplace mantel. Mia used to love decorating this room and the rest of the main floor for Christmas. Candles, evergreen branches, lace snowflakes and ribbons—she went all out for the holidays. He could almost smell the cinnamon and cloves from a concoction she'd simmer on the stove.

Without Mia's touch, the house had no life. No wonder Bill had told him to get the decorations out.

Lord, I want to make Christmas nice for Noah, but I don't know how. I mean, I bought him presents. But this house? I can't bear to open the bins with Mia's ornaments. What do I do?

The alarm went off.

He was already regretting tomorrow's Christmas tree excursion—why had he asked Brittany to go with them? He should have just cut one down with Noah. They didn't need her help.

But he kind of did need her help. And not for her skills cutting down a tree. He'd asked her because she'd been his friend. His best friend before Mia. And lately he felt lost.

Next year, she'd be in California and he'd get through

the holidays fine on his own. But this year, he needed a little help.

And if Brittany was the one to give it to him, he'd swallow his pride and his fears and take it. Even if it threatened to melt the tundra over his heart.

'Tis the season to be...worried. Fa-la-la-la...

Brittany sat at Nan's kitchen table and checked another item off the list. She'd spent all morning trying to track down information. She'd asked Nan about how she paid her bills, and to her relief, Nan had gotten out her checkbook and the shoebox where she kept the invoices. As soon as the bills arrived, Nan filled out the checks so she wouldn't misplace them. There were a few late notices in the shoebox, but from what Brittany could tell, they'd been paid, too. All in all, the system gave her some peace of mind.

Then Brittany had asked her when she'd last had a physical. Nan couldn't remember, so they'd set up an appointment for Thursday morning.

What if the doctor told her Nan had Alzheimer's? Or something else? Something terminal?

Stop assuming the worst! Ugh! She was getting to be like her mother! And nothing pleased that woman.

Brittany still regretted telling her mom she'd decided to open a dance studio instead of continuing to audition for professional gigs. Her mother had coldly asked her why she was wasting her life. Brittany had gotten defensive and blurted out her plans to put together a competitive dance team. It had pacified her mother, but the encounter still made her feel nauseous all these years later.

If she'd known then how much blood, sweat and tears it would take to get her own studio, would she have gone forward with her plan?

She stretched out her legs to relieve some of the tension, but her nerves were all janky and tight.

Why hadn't the bank called yet? She swiped her phone and found the loan officer's number. She called it, but it went to voice mail. After leaving a brief message, she hung up.

God, please let them approve the line of credit. I've sacrificed so much for this.

The sound of an engine caught her attention. Mason must be here. She peeked out the window. Yep. He was parking his truck. She couldn't tear her eyes away as he got out, then unbuckled Noah from the back seat. As soon as his feet touched the ground, the child ran toward the porch. Mason followed with long, sure strides. Brittany could watch the man all day long.

"Nan!" Noah's voice carried from the porch.

Nan pushed herself up from the recliner.

"I'll get the door." Brittany jogged over to the entrance. "Well, look who's here. How are you doing today, Mr. Noah?"

"I'm not a mister, Miss Bwittany." He shook his head in a serious manner, tearing off his coat, gloves and boots.

"You're not?"

"No, that's Daddy, silly." He ran to Nan and hugged her knees. "Nan!"

"Noah." She stroked his hair. "I'll get the cookies."

"Howdy." Mason entered, stomping his boots on the mat. "I've got a meeting tonight, so we can only stay for a few minutes."

"That's fine, honey. It's good to see you." Nan leaned in for a hug before shuffling to the kitchen with Noah's hand in hers.

Brittany met his eyes. Being alone with him tangled

her stomach into knots. She shifted from one foot to the other. "How was your day?"

"Cold." He took off his boots, looking up at her as he did. "We moved the herd to a different pasture. The snow on my face felt like ice shards."

"Really? I've always thought of snow as gentle and fluffy."

"Not when you're on horseback and the wind's kicking up." He hitched his chin to the kitchen. "How's she doing?"

"Good. She's good." She made a flourishing movement with her hand. "It's weird, you know? Being here. Slowing down. Our winter recital was last week and every night was super crammed. But now I have all the time in the world and then some. It's a big change from my normal routine, especially since I'd been taking extra shifts at the diner to afford this time off. Did you know waitressing is a lot like dancing?" She couldn't seem to stop talking. Where was an off button when she needed one?

"I did not know that."

"It is. They both have a rhythm. Fast, slow, steady, pirouette, hold the tray steady and when it's all over, ouch, my lower back." Why was she telling him all this? *Stop babbling!*

"Okay, what's wrong?" He looked at her with a concerned expression.

"Wrong? Nothing's wrong. What are you talking about?"

"You're rambling. What's bothering you?"

She sighed. "Nan has a doctor's appointment on Thursday."

"And you're worried about what you'll hear." He kept his voice low.

"Yup." He got it. He'd always gotten her.

"I'd tell you not to sweat it, but…" He wiped his palm down his cheek. "Sometimes you hear bad news. Nothing you can do to stop it from coming."

She swallowed, knowing he was right, yet wishing he was wrong.

"Can I give you some advice?" he asked. "Enjoy her now."

Three words that cut right through her heart.

But the bank and the studio and Nan's memory lapses and her refusal to shower…

He took a seat at the table and she did, too. Nan and Noah approached with the treats. She couldn't choke down a cookie if she tried. Thankfully, Noah launched into an explanation of how to hold scissors. Auntie Eden had let him use safety scissors that morning.

When the boy stopped talking long enough to take a drink of milk, Mason addressed Nan. "I don't know if Brittany told you, but I recently found out I have a brother."

"A brother?" The creases in her forehead deepened. "No, that can't be right. Gus and Beth would have told me."

Brittany glanced at Nan, then Mason.

"It was a surprise to me, too," he said.

"Are you sure you have a brother?" Nan asked. "How old is he?"

"We're the same age. Twins. Identical. And yes, I'm sure. There's no mistaking it."

"Twins, you say?" She blinked a few times and shook her head in wonder. "No, I guess there wouldn't be any mistaking it."

Brittany had nothing to add so she let her toes draw patterns on the floor under the table.

"I can't believe they could have kept it a secret." Nan gazed at the wall. "I knew John and Lisa were having a baby. Beth confided it to me when she found out. But I didn't know you had been born until after the car crash and they brought you back here for good."

"Did you know anything else about my parents? Or how Ma and Pops felt about them?"

A faraway look glazed over her eyes. Brittany knew that look, and it meant Mason wouldn't be getting answers. Not from Nan, at least.

"Gus loved John," Nan said. "He rode him pretty hard, though. Had high expectations."

Brittany straightened. Maybe she'd been wrong about Nan.

"John was supposed to join Gus at the ranch and take it over eventually, but he was a thoughtful boy. Liked reading and studying." Nan smiled. "Oh, he liked riding horses and working cattle, too. I thought a lot of that boy. Sometimes I hoped he would marry my Joanie. Thought he'd be good for her—to ground her a bit. But after high school, he got in an awful row with his folks. Lasted all summer. And then he was gone. He'd gotten a scholarship to study in Colorado. Gus and Beth didn't talk much about him after that."

"What about the wedding? Whenever I asked Ma and Pops about my parents, they got real tight-lipped."

"John and Lisa eloped. Got married in a courthouse. Broke your grandma's heart, and it didn't help that Gus blamed Lisa for stealing John from his rightful place on the ranch."

Brittany cringed. The picture Nan was painting was sad. Really sad.

"Did John and Lisa ever come back here?" Brittany asked Nan.

"I seem to recall them coming back once for a visit, but I don't remember for sure."

Mason wore a pensive expression. Noah was munching on cookies, quietly taking it all in.

"You knew my grandparents as well as anyone." Mason leaned forward. "Why would they come home with one baby? And never mention I had a twin?"

The brightness in Nan's cheeks faded. "They must have reckoned it was for the best."

"For whom?" His voice rose.

"I don't know. They made the best decisions they could at the time. I did the same with Joanie. Maybe we both were wrong."

Brittany went still. Why would Nan think she'd done anything wrong with Brittany's mom, Joan?

"Can we feed the kitties now?" Noah pleaded, his cookie eaten.

"We can only stay out there for five minutes, Noah." Mason sounded stern.

"Yes, go feed them, honey. I'm a bit tired." Nan looked spent.

"Why don't you take a nap?" Brittany stood and helped Nan to her feet. Mason and Noah were putting on their coats.

"I think I will." She patted Brittany's arm. "Go out with the boys. Have some fun."

An entire notebook full of questions came to mind, but she simply kissed Nan's cheek. "I will."

She'd never thought much about the relationship between her mother and Nan. Brittany hadn't talked to her mom in forever. They weren't close.

Brittany put on her boots and outerwear and followed Mason and Noah to the barn. As Noah rushed forward trying to catch snowflakes on his tongue, Mason held back to walk with her.

"I'm sorry she didn't have more information for you." Brittany glanced at his profile.

"Don't be." He gave her a quick sideways glance. "I didn't know Pops blamed my mother for my dad not ranching. It's good to have more details—anything, really—about my parents."

"Have you talked to Ryder lately?" She kept pace with him in the snow.

"Yeah. I called him last night. We're both trying to learn anything we can about our pasts."

"Any progress?"

"I found a picture of my dad when he was a little older than Noah. Looked just like him. Made me want to find pictures of me at that age. Ma wasn't very organized, though."

"Aw, I'd love to see the picture. That is, if you don't mind."

They approached the barn. He slid the door open and Noah surged inside.

"I don't mind." He stood a few feet from her, but they might as well have been touching. The connection they'd had as kids, as teens, roared back, and she caught her breath, wanting to fall into it. To fall into him.

"Push me, Miss Bwittany!"

The moment shattered. It was just as well. She was used to standing on her own two feet and Christmas vacation wasn't reality. Falling into him meant giving up on things she wanted. She was too close to finally getting the studio and dance team she'd dreamed about. She wouldn't do something stupid, not this time around.

"Okay, spill it all." Gabby shut the door of the private meeting room at Mountain View Inn at seven o'clock on the dot that night. "How is it going with you and Ryder?"

Eden, sitting in a comfy chair, watched him expectantly.

Every Tuesday the three of them met here. Gabby,

concerned about him and Eden in the months after Mia died, had started the group so they could support each other and study God's word. Mason admired Gabby's go-to spirit even in the face of her own tragedy this year. Although Gabby mourned her sister, she never seemed to be in danger of falling apart. Or maybe she was good at hiding it—like he was.

"What happened to opening with a prayer?" Sitting on the couch, he propped one ankle on the other knee. The leather couch faced a tall stone fireplace. An antler chandelier hung above them. Bookshelves lined the walls on either side of the fireplace. The cozy seating area took up one section of the room, and a conference table took up the rest.

Gabby sank into the love seat opposite and leveled a death stare his way. "Your texts have been uninformative."

"Okay, okay." He held out his palms. "Ryder and I are talking. Trying to figure out why we never knew about each other. We haven't found many answers." He filled them in on what he knew.

"So who is older?" Gabby asked.

"Me. He's the baby."

"I'm sure you're already lording it over him."

He shot her a cocky grin.

Eden smiled and lowered her gaze.

"Did you ever just kind of know you had a twin?" Gabby scooted to the edge of her seat. "Did you sense it?"

"No. Wish I could say I did. I don't know what he's thinking or feeling. I really don't know much about him at all. He's coming to stay for a while over Christmas break, though."

"That's great!" Gabby slapped the arm of the couch.

"Anyway, enough about me. Let's get this meeting

started." Mason figured he'd take the initiative this week. "Let's pray."

"Fine, you're off the hook for now…"

They all bowed their heads.

"Dear Father, thank You for another week. Please help us heal our wounds and trust You to take care of Mia and Allison for us. Amen."

"Amen," the women echoed.

"I…ah…have been fighting some uncomfortable feelings this week." Mason felt the heat rushing up his neck. Exposing his emotions was hard for him.

"I would think so." Gabby nodded.

"About Ryder?" Eden fixed her gaze on him.

"Yes." His conscience blasted him. The whole point of this group was to be honest with each other in order to heal. And if he couldn't tell them what was really going on, what kind of friend was he? "Well, Ryder is part of it."

"What do you mean?" Gabby's face screwed up.

"The feelings have to do with the person he showed up with. Gabby, you didn't grow up here, but Eden, you might remember Brittany Green." So far, so good, even if he couldn't read Eden's expression. "She and I were friends growing up. But we had a falling-out a long time ago. When she showed up last week, it was like taking sandpaper to a raw wound. I hated seeing her on my porch. Especially with a man who looked just like me."

"Especially?" Eden asked quietly. "Why?"

"I don't know." He blew out a breath. "It brought up things I didn't want to think about. We'd dated briefly."

"Mia never told me about her." Eden didn't sound upset, just curious.

"It happened a few years before Mia and I started dating."

"So your old flame shows up with the twin you didn't

know you had…" Gabby's cheeks puffed out before she exhaled. She shook her head. "Ouch."

"I'm only telling you this because seeing her made me realize how much I resent the fact Mia isn't here anymore. I had to meet Ryder by myself."

"But you weren't by yourself," Eden said. "Brittany was there."

"I think what he means is that Mia was his best friend and she wasn't there at a time when he needed her." Gabby shifted to sit on one leg.

"Exactly." He nodded.

"Mia's gone, Mason." Eden reached over and squeezed his hand. He squeezed it back. He really liked his sister-in-law.

"I know." He sighed. "That's why we're here, right? Anyway, I'm doing better."

"Whenever you get those raw feelings, pray." Eden smiled.

"I will." He took a moment to compose himself. "What about you guys? What's going on?"

"Just trying to get through the holidays." Gabby deflated. "I can't believe Allison is gone. I keep checking my phone for texts and thinking about Christmas gifts for her—but then this awful, crushing sadness descends on me. Honestly, if it wasn't for the baby, I don't think I'd get out of bed."

"Do you think you're depressed?" Eden asked.

"Maybe. A little. If I didn't have Phoebe to take care of, I would be a mess. The baby needs me, needs a mama. I have to keep it together for her sake."

"You're a great mom, Gabby." Eden got up and gave her a hug.

Mason would never say it, but he envied them their physical affection. They comforted each other with hugs all the time. He'd shied away from embraces since Mia's death, and he missed it sometimes. Missed having caring arms around him.

"Still no word on Phoebe's dad?" Mason broached the topic gingerly. Gabby's sister had a one-night stand down in Texas, which had resulted in Phoebe. Allison had tracked down his address and sent multiple letters, but never heard from the guy. After Allison's death, Gabby had continued to try to contact him.

"No, and Lord forgive me, but I hope it stays that way. I couldn't bear the thought of him coming in here and taking the baby from me."

He didn't like the idea of a child growing up without a father, but he couldn't fault Gabby. She'd done everything in her power to alert the baby's daddy.

"What about you, Eden?" Mason gave her his most tender smile. In many ways, she was the mommy Noah no longer had. "How are you holding up?"

"Okay. The holidays are hard." Her face fell.

"I hope you know how much I appreciate all you do for Noah. Every day he comes home brimming with news about all the fun stuff he did with Auntie Eden."

"He's my sunshine, Mason." Her smile brightened her eyes. "I love him. I'm thankful to be part of his life."

"You'll always be part of his life."

She raised her eyebrows slightly, then looked away. Strange. What did that mean?

"Let's get back into our study of Psalm 37." Gabby opened her Bible.

Mason opened his Bible and said a silent prayer. *Lord, thank You for this group. I would have sunk long ago if it wasn't for these two women.*

As he trailed his finger down the page, he couldn't get

Eden's words out of his mind. *You weren't by yourself. Brittany was there.*

Eden didn't get it. He'd needed Mia there, not Brittany. Although now that she'd shown up, he didn't hate her anymore. And that was dangerous.

He'd lost her once.

He'd lost his wife for good.

His heart couldn't take loving and losing again.

Chapter Six

Late Wednesday morning, after doing a bit of Christmas shopping, Brittany sat with Nan at a cozy table for two near the fireplace in Cattle Drive Coffee. Being in Rendezvous had piqued her curiosity about things she'd refused to dwell on in the past. Like her mother. Last night she'd asked Nan about her mom, and she'd shared detailed stories of "her Joanie" growing up.

Why had Nan and Mom grown apart? As far as Brittany knew, they spoke only a couple of times a year for birthdays and Christmas, and they were brief phone calls. Basically, it seemed like the same strained relationship she had with her mom. She'd never lived up to her mother's expectations, so no big surprise there. But Nan? The sweetest woman on the planet? Why would Mom shun her, too?

"I'm glad you and Mason have been spending time together, dear." Nan stirred her coffee.

"Me, too." And, shockingly, she was. When she'd arrived in town with Ryder, she'd fully expected to get a blistering lecture from Mason followed by stone-cold silence. Instead, she'd gotten a slow thaw of their former friendship. Not that it could be anything more—but to be on speaking terms with him again meant a lot to her. "I'm going with him this afternoon to pick out a Christmas tree. I'm getting one for us, too."

"That will be lovely." Nan took a tentative sip and set the cup back on the table. "Oh, that's hot. He's been different since his wife died."

"I imagine it was very painful to watch his wife suffer."

"He was happy when he was with her. I'd see them horseback riding together at the edge of the property sometimes. And she would stop in with freshly baked muffins now and then. I liked Mia. Very much."

A flash of jealousy tightened her chest. A part of her itched to change the subject, but another part wanted to learn everything she could about his wife.

"What was she like?" Brittany raised her mug and blew on the surface before attempting a sip. *Mmm...delicious.*

"Mia?" Nan looked off to the side with a smile. "She was tall. On the quiet side. Kind. Very kind. Everyone liked her. I don't think I ever heard anyone say a bad word about her."

She shrank in her seat. Tall, quiet, kind? The exact opposite of herself.

"Did she have a job before she had Noah?"

Nan shook her head. "No, she helped Mason with the ranch. She kept the ranch's books. She loved to cook and bake. Mason had a fine wife in her. My heart broke for him when she got the diagnosis."

"What kind of cancer did she have?"

"I... I don't recall. But it took her quick."

Horrible. Mia sounded like the perfect wife for Mason. A real partner. Something Brittany would never be. Teaching kids and teens how to dance brought her joy.

Staying in a farmhouse all day, baking, keeping ranch records and occasionally riding horses with a husband didn't appeal to her.

Except…thinking of Mason's broad shoulders, light brown eyes, his laugh, the comfort of being with him… well, if he was the rancher, it appealed more than she wanted to admit.

But she couldn't imagine a life without dance.

If she could scoop up Mason and Noah and set them in Santa Ana…

Really, Brit? Like that would ever happen. He'd hate California. Wyoming was where he belonged. And she'd be wise to think about something else.

"Nan, why do you think Mom is so distant?" She watched her intently. She didn't seem flustered, but a frown deepened the lines in her face.

"I reckon life didn't turn out the way she wanted." Nan met her gaze and Brittany acknowledged the truth of the statement. "As a little girl, Joanie was always seeing the bright side of things, but she'd see them as too bright. Overly optimistic to the point where she couldn't help but be disappointed."

It was her turn to frown. That didn't sound like Mom at all. Her mother was a pragmatic realist. She always had something negative to say about Brittany's life and plans. That's why Brittany had stopped sharing them with her.

"Howdy, Ada." An elderly couple approached. "Is this your granddaughter?"

Nan's expression glazed over. Brittany's stomach clenched. Her grandmother didn't seem to recognize these two. Not wanting her to be embarrassed, she held out her hand. "I'm Brittany Green, her granddaughter. I used to spend my summers in Rendezvous."

"Oh, that's right," the white-haired lady said. "My, you've grown up. Do you remember Brittany, Dan?"

The wiry man wore typical ranch gear—a Stetson, work jacket, jeans and cowboy boots. "You ran around with Mason Fanning, didn't you? I used to see you kids together in town. You always looked like you were having fun."

"Did you hear he has a twin?" The woman leaned over and widened her eyes. "Identical."

"I did hear that, actually."

"Where are my manners? I'm Ginger Bates, and this is my husband, Dan. We live on the other side of Rendezvous. Dan worked with your grandfather."

Brittany glanced at Nan, who seemed herself once more.

"We won't keep you. Just wanted to say howdy." Ginger waved to them both and took Dan by the arm before leaving.

"He used to work with Grandpa?"

"Who?" Nan averted her gaze and drank her coffee.

"Dan Bates. The man who just stopped by."

"Oh, yes. Neil hired him at the feed company. Dan was a good worker."

She sighed. One step forward, two steps back. She hoped the doctor would give them some answers tomorrow. Because the way Nan went in and out of remembering things, Brittany didn't have much peace of mind at the present.

"What do you mean we're not going to a tree farm?" Brittany sounded shocked.

"Tree farm? What gave you that idea?" Mason glanced at her sitting in the passenger side of his truck Wednesday afternoon. The tight quarters carried the scent of her light perfume. The way his nerves were jangling, he felt like he was eighteen again.

Eighteen? Yeah, right. You're a long way from eighteen. The rearview showed Noah strapped into the car seat in the back. His eyelids had grown droopy. No surprise there. He usually took a short nap around this time.

"I thought everyone got real trees from a farm."

"Maybe in Hallmark movies but not around here." The truck bumped along the path. "Why would I buy a tree when we can cut one down on my property?"

"Wait." She held her arm out. Her white jacket was probably warm, but the color wasn't practical. Around these parts, everything got dirty. And he couldn't help noticing the gray gloves she wore wouldn't keep her fingers warm for long. "We're cutting one down?"

"Yeah. What did you think I meant?"

"I don't know. I guess I figured we'd pick out precut trees the way most people do where I live."

"Precut? You can't be serious. Is that what you do?"

"No." Her pretty white teeth flashed in a grin. "I have an artificial."

"Artificial." He shook his head, pretending disgust. "You don't get the evergreen smell from an artificial tree."

"You also don't get needles and sap and the hassle of getting rid of it in January."

"True. But it's worth it." His 4x4 handled the dirt path through the hills like a champ. "We're fortunate there are only a few inches of snow, or we might have had trouble getting to the northeast section of my land."

"Is that where you've tucked your Christmas tree farm? Please tell me there will be a hot chocolate stand."

"No hot chocolate stand, but I brought a thermos and some cups." He almost hadn't brought the hot chocolate, but Noah had insisted and he wanted to make the outing fun for him.

"My hero." She made a production out of fluttering her eyelashes. Her face reminded him of a summer day. Happy, bright and full of joy.

Heat crept up his cheeks. He was no one's hero. Not anymore.

"Tell me about the ranch," Brittany said. "What's it like owning the property you grew up on?"

"It's great." He maneuvered around a tight curve and continued forward. Well, it used to be great. Back when Mia would get up with him while it was dark. She'd make coffee, and if it wasn't too snowy, she'd ride out with him on the feed truck and help open gates. They'd never said much. They didn't have to.

"Did you change anything? Besides remodeling the house, that is."

"No." He'd been ready to—had planned on expanding the herd. Then Mia had gotten pregnant, and they'd decided to wait until they could save more money. It was a good thing they had, or his current financial situation would be even worse. She'd found out she had cervical cancer at her first appointment with the obstetrician.

How many times had he wondered if their decision to delay treatment until after Noah was born had been a fatal mistake?

God, help me let the guilt go.

Brittany faced the windshield, and he noted the way her hands moved in patterns ever so slightly on her legs. He'd forgotten that habit of hers.

"What about you?" he asked. "Dancing professionally didn't do it for you? Is that why you're teaching dance?"

"Yes and no." Her chin tilted upward, not in defiance, but in honesty. "There are a million dancers with big dreams, and I realized after a few years of auditioning, the chances of me making it were slim to none. So I started teaching. I love it, but renting rehearsal space limits my options. I need my own studio."

"So get one." The stand of evergreens appeared. He slowed the truck.

"I'm trying." The words were so quiet, he had to peek at her to make sure she'd said them.

"What's stopping you?" He cut the engine and pocketed the keys.

"I take it we're here." She opened her door and climbed down. He wouldn't press her. Didn't really care if she had a studio or not. Made no difference in his life.

He unbuckled Noah, who sprang awake as quickly as a jack-in-the-box. "Christmas tree?"

"Yep." He set Noah on the ground. Brittany had shoved her hands in her pockets and was shivering near the front of the truck. The pensive expression on her face pulled at his heart.

Maybe he did care if she had a studio or not. Maybe it bothered him—just a little bit—that she wasn't as happy as he'd always imagined.

He hauled the metal bow saw along with a chain saw out of the back of the truck, then approached her. "The studio's important, huh?"

"It is." She stared up at him, and he had to look away from those shimmering eyes. "With my own space, I could hire more dance teachers, attract more students and finally put together a competitive dance team. But properties are so expensive where I live."

"Can you take out a loan?" He started walking toward the row of tall pines. Noah scampered ahead.

"I'm waiting to hear back from a bank who might be willing to give me a business line of credit. For what it's worth, I've applied several times to various banks over the past couple of years with no success."

"This time will be different."

"What if it isn't?"

"You'll find a way to make it happen. I know you. You're…tenacious." He checked to make sure Noah was nearby. The kid was running toward the trees. "Hey, slow down, buckaroo."

"I'm gonna find us the biggest one, Daddy!"

"Rule number one. It needs to fit in our house." He broke into a light jog. Brittany's laugh filled the air. She'd tossed her head back and was gazing up at the sky. Her delight made him halt in his tracks.

She was joyous and full of life. She took his breath away.

His pulse raced out of control, and it annoyed him. Because he didn't get all jittery around women. Not anymore.

She lifted her leg, bent it and did some sort of spinning move. Right there in the snow under the blue sky.

Who did that? Who danced in the snow?

He lurched ahead, following the trail of boot prints Noah was making. His torso felt hot, and it wasn't due to the physical activity. Brittany was tropical sun on his face after a cold winter. She was fireworks on the Fourth of July.

She was pure excitement to him. Always had been.

"It's cold, but it's perfect." She caught up to him. "Listen. It's so quiet. I didn't know how peaceful it could be in the winter."

He shifted the chain saw to his other hand. "You're used to Rendezvous in the summer."

"It's not like I've never seen snow, but—" she looked up and around "—this is special. Is that a hawk?"

"An eagle. The white head gives it away."

"Daddy! I see a pwonghorn." Noah spun to face them, pointing to the left.

"Good eye, buddy. That's a deer."

"I found a deer, Miss Bwittany!"

"Wow! I don't think I've ever seen one so close." The deer took off running, its white tail bobbing as it disappeared into the forest ahead of them.

"Let's go this way." Mason directed Noah to the left where rows of spruce and fir trees stood.

The boy slowed as he came to the first tree. "What about this one?"

"It's got a hole." Mason strolled around it, pointing to a bare section. "We'll keep looking."

"Ooh, this one's big." Noah stared up way above them at a blue spruce.

"Aah…it's a little too big." Mason gestured for him to keep going.

"But I like it, Daddy!"

"I know, but it's too tall. Remember the rule we made?"

His face fell. "It has to fit in the house."

"Right."

"Hey, Mason?" Brittany had stopped near a short, fluffy Fraser fir. "Do you think this would be okay for Nan?"

Noah raced to her and imitated his daddy as he inspected it. "Nan needs a big one."

"This is pretty big." Brittany framed her chin between her thumb and index finger. "I think it would look good in her front window. What do you think?"

"I think she'd love it," Mason said.

"I think she'd love it, too." Noah jumped up and down. "Can I help cut it?"

"Not this time, buckaroo." He set the chain saw on the

ground and started trimming the lower branches from the tree trunk with the bow saw. "Okay, stand back."

He waited until Brittany had hauled Noah close to her, keeping her hands on his tiny shoulders, before starting the chain saw. The buzzing sound filled the air, and in no time flat, he'd cut down the tree. He switched the saw off. "What's next?"

"You did it!" Noah clapped his hands.

After dragging it to the tree line near the truck, they resumed looking at the spruces. Brittany told him about taking Nan out for coffee this morning.

"She didn't seem to recognize Ginger and Dan Bates." Her easy strides matched his as they followed Noah from tree to tree. "I don't remember them, either. I guess Dan worked with my grandpa. I have to admit, I don't recognize many people around here anymore."

"You'd recognize Babs O'Rourke," he said dryly.

"The redhead who knew everything?" She chuckled. "I'm surprised she's still around."

"She owns the inn in town where my friend Gabby works. Still as nosy as ever."

"Maybe she would know something about your past."

He'd like to think so, but he knew better. "Nah, she would have said something by now."

"Too bad. Oh, look at this tree!" Brittany stopped near a stunner. "Someone around here must know something. Your dad would have had friends, classmates, right?"

"I suppose." His neck craned up. "Hey, Noah, what do you think?"

"It's big!" Noah ran to him.

"Then I'll cut it down." As he repeated the steps he'd taken with the fir, his mind kept tripping over Brittany's words. His father would have had friends here. He'd grown up in Rendezvous. Maybe she was onto something.

Before starting the chain saw, he peered back. Brittany had picked up Noah, and he was chatting in his animated way. They made a striking picture. Like a mother and child.

Instantly, his thoughts went to Mia. It was as though a foot of snow got dumped on his head. Noah wasn't Brittany's child.

Mason started the chain saw with more force than necessary. His connection with Brittany might still be there, but that didn't make it right.

He'd been wrong to spend this time with her. Wrong to talk and be open with her.

The saw sliced through the trunk of the tree. He wished he could make the same clean break with Brittany.

Christmas was next week. Then she'd leave. And in the meantime, he'd keep his mind where it belonged— on making a nice Christmas for Noah, taking care of the ranch and finding out why he and Ryder had been separated.

On anything but Brittany Green.

"You'll help us decorate, won't you?" Nan asked Noah and Mason.

Brittany glanced at Mason stringing the multicolored lights around the tree. The set of his jaw told her he had no intention of staying. He'd been quiet ever since they had their hot chocolate after cutting down the trees. She didn't know why his mood had changed. But she was glad he'd offered to set up Nan's tree—she herself had no clue how to do it.

"Yes!" Noah dug both hands into the garlands of silver tinsel and tossed them into the air, giggling all the while. His joy was contagious and Brittany couldn't help but chuckle.

"Can I put the candy canes on?" Noah eyed the box of candy canes sitting on the end table.

"I don't see why not." Nan returned to her recliner to watch their progress.

Brittany waited for Mason to let Nan down easy, but to her surprise, he didn't.

"What's next?" As he reached to push a light strand over a branch, his gray Henley strained against his chest muscles, and his sinewy forearms flexed. He smelled good—too good—like pine and masculine bodywash. Her insides had been dancing *The Nutcracker* for hours.

"Um…bulbs?" A part of her wished he would have declined Nan's invitation to decorate. His presence was throwing her off balance.

He made her feel things she didn't want to feel.

When he'd said *You'll find a way to make it happen*, the words had wrapped around her like a cozy blanket. It had been a long, long time since anyone had believed in her.

Usually when she confided to friends about her dreams, they meant to be supportive but gave unintentionally hurtful advice. Her last boyfriend had told her to relocate to a different area or find another career. Her friend Angie had been encouraging, but at the same time had warned her not to waste her entire life in the pursuit of a studio. Then Angie had gotten married, moved to Texas and had a baby. They weren't as close as they used to be. Just one in a long line of friends who'd moved on with marriage, career and family.

"Can I get through?" Mason pointed to the bins. She stepped aside. He lifted a box of old glass bulbs in a variety of colors. "These okay?"

"Go for it." Other things about today disturbed her,

too. Like how free and unencumbered it felt to be outside in the wild of Wyoming. And how nice it was to hike down rows of Christmas trees without rushing or worrying about getting to her next job on time.

The pace of this place was growing on her. And that scared her.

She didn't know who she was without the promise of the competitive dance team. She supposed she was a small-time dance instructor, a waitress and a data entry clerk. Real impressive.

"What are those, Miss Bwittany?" Noah leaned against her shoulder and pointed to a baggie full of plastic reindeer.

"I remember these." She held up the bag so Nan could see them. "We bought them at a Christmas-in-July sale. Do you remember, Nan?"

"Oh, yes. Hill Country Store had good clearances. It's too bad it shut down."

"When did it go out of business?" She opened the baggie and handed a reindeer to Noah. He hung it on a branch.

"I don't remember." Nan looked pensive.

"It's no big deal."

"My memory isn't as good as it used to be."

"We'll mention it to the doctor tomorrow." She'd told Nan about the appointment a few times, but Nan kept forgetting.

"The doctor? I'm fine. No need to fuss."

"I'm not fussing." She handed Noah another reindeer. "It's a physical."

"Oh." She wrung her hands. "There's no need. I'm not sick."

"It won't take long." Brittany kept her voice soft, gentle, but this exchange reminded her a little too much of the struggles she'd had with Nan over showering. When her grandmother didn't want to do something, it was difficult to get her to budge.

"If I remember correctly, Hill Country Store shut down about five years ago." Mason poked his head around the tree. "The dollar store replaced it."

"That's right." Nan nodded.

"I like the dollar store." Noah took a break from the reindeer to hang four candy canes on one branch. "Grandpa gets me horses and cars from there."

"Horses and cars? I'd like those." Brittany winked at him. "Dollar stores are fun."

"I'll show them to you. I have a lot—" he stretched out his arms wide "—of horses and cars. Come to my house and you can see. You can decorate our tree with us."

The flicker in Mason's cheek told her he didn't love the idea. *That makes two of us.* She lowered her head, pretending to fix a hook on one of the reindeer. In all the years she'd been teaching dance, she'd never once wavered about her goal.

Until today.

Seeing that eagle soaring above them after Mason's encouragement had taken away the urgency of her plans.

She'd had the sensation of freedom.

But Rendezvous—Mason—wasn't freedom. It was giving up.

"That's so nice of you, Noah," she said brightly. "But decorating your tree is a special activity for you and your daddy."

"You could come, too." He sidled up to her and touched her hair. "You're pwetty."

The precious little boy. She could scoop him up and tuck him in her pocket, he was that cute.

"Actually, I thought Auntie Eden and Grandma and

Grandpa might want to help us decorate." Mason hung another bulb on the tree. His expression gave nothing away.

"Miss Bwittany can help."

"Not this time, buckaroo." His cell phone rang and he excused himself. She watched him stride toward the kitchen, the low tones of his voice fading.

At least the need for distance was mutual.

"Look at these!" She held up a pair of mice wearing elf hats to Noah. "Do you want to hang them up?"

"Yes!" He stretched to hook one near the middle of the tree. "I don't like real mouses. They're naughty."

"I don't like real ones, either. If I see one, I scream." She crouched down on her knees to find more ornaments.

"I'd save you from them." Noah touched her hair again.

He was too sweet. "Thank you. If I saw a mouse, I'd need your protection."

He threw his little arms around her neck and hugged her. Her heart melted.

Mason came back into the room and his gaze darkened as he saw them hug.

"That was Ryder. He was able to adjust his schedule. He and the girls are coming in on Friday."

"That's great." Brittany rose and took a step toward him. He stepped back.

She froze, doing her best to keep her smile on her face.

Their truce had defrosted their relationship, but it didn't mean things could go back to the way they were.

Mason wasn't interested in her. Not anymore.

And she'd be wise not to forget it.

Chapter Seven

❧

"I'm concerned about my grandmother." Brittany joined Doctor Landson in a small office at the clinic late Thursday morning. He'd finished examining Nan, and a nurse was helping her fill out paperwork at the desk. "She forgets things I tell her—sometimes within hours—and gets confused easily. She's not bathing regularly, and she's lost weight."

"I've been taking care of Ada for years." The older man scanned the forms in his hands. "She's slowing down, but that's to be expected at her age. I do an informal test on my elderly patients to check mental functioning. It's conversational. I ask a few questions about their week and about the past. Your grandmother has some short-term memory loss and maybe mild cognitive impairment."

"How serious is it?"

"If you're worried about dementia, she'd be in the earliest stages."

Dementia. The word Brittany had been dreading. "If she does have dementia, what are her options? How quickly does it progress?"

"It depends on what's causing it and on the individual. I don't see marked changes in her mental functioning from the last time I examined her. If you're worried, though, I can order an MRI. She'd have to go to the city for it. I can refer you to a neurologist if you'd like."

"What would an MRI do?" She didn't think Nan would agree to an appointment in the city.

"It would show if she had a stroke, bleeding, a tumor or other complications."

"Why haven't you already ordered one?"

"Your grandmother has no physical complaints leading me to believe she needs an MRI."

The thought comforted her, but there was still one question nagging. "Do you think she needs to live in a nursing home?"

He frowned. "In my opinion, no. If you're concerned about her hygiene and eating habits, you could hire a home health aide to come in once or twice a week. She could look into assisted-living homes, too. We have a few in the area."

Brittany relaxed a bit. Everything the doctor was saying made sense. Plus, he had a way of speaking that put her at ease.

"What if she refused to move into an assisted-living facility?"

"Do you have power of attorney?" He leaned forward, his forearms on the desk and hands lightly clasped.

"No."

"In that case, there's not much you can do. Talk to her. You can always make an appointment with an attorney to discuss her legal options."

"Thank you. This has helped me more than you know."

"My pleasure." He rose and shook her hand.

She moved to the door but turned back. "Are there any home health aides you could recommend?"

"We have several in the community. Do you know

Gabby Stover? She works at Mountain View Inn. She hired help for her grandmother. She might be able to recommend someone."

"Thank you." Gabby Stover. Hadn't she heard that name before? She'd pop over to the inn later to get some information. Maybe hiring a home health aide would be the best solution for the time being.

Brittany exited the room and put her arm around Nan's shoulders. "Are you ready?"

Nan looked flustered. She held several sheets of paper, and a nurse told her they would call with the blood test results later in the week.

"Here, I'll take those while you button your coat." Brittany took the papers. "Let's get some lunch. I'm hungry. Where should we go?"

One of the ladies behind the counter smiled at them. "Riverview Lounge has homemade lunch specials on weekdays."

"Thanks." Brittany hooked her arm in Nan's. "I don't think I've been there. Should we try it?"

"I'd like that." Nan patted Brittany's hand.

After getting directions to the restaurant, she steered Nan outside. The wind plastered her hair against her face as she helped her grandmother into the truck. The white sky matched the white ground. Dreary.

She drove over the bridge, crossing Silver Rocks River, and into downtown Rendezvous. Soon, they were hurrying into Riverview Lounge. A blast of warm air and lively conversations greeted them inside.

As soon as they'd settled into a booth near the back, Brittany broached the subject she knew needed to be discussed. She couldn't put it off forever and now was as good a time as any.

"Nan, have you done any long-term planning?"

"What do you mean?" She folded her coat and placed it next to her on the booth. A waiter stopped by to tell them the daily special, took their orders and promised to be right back with their drinks.

"If anything were to happen to you, who would pay your bills? Or help you make medical decisions?"

"Nothing's going to happen to me, dear." She lightly rubbed her bony hands together in an attempt to warm up.

"Have you given any thought to appointing a power of attorney?" She tried to keep her tone light, but she felt brittle enough to snap.

"Attorney? No, I don't need a lawyer." Her pursed lips and rigid back didn't bode well for continuing the conversation.

"It's for planning purposes. Like, say, in the event you fell and broke a hip. You wouldn't be able to pay your bills if you were in the hospital. And what if you were unconscious? Who would make decisions for you?"

"Mason always takes care of me, honey." Nan's expression softened. "I don't want you worrying."

"But legally—"

"I'm fine. I've always paid my bills, and if I fall, I fall. Mason will get me to the hospital."

The waiter arrived with two coffees and waters. Brittany smiled her thanks, then watched Nan pour two creamers and a packet of sugar in her coffee. What now? She couldn't force her to get on board with long-term planning.

Her foot bounced on the floor, a sign she was anxious. Maybe a different approach would get Nan to budge.

"Do you ever get lonely?" She raised her mug, holding it between her hands. The rising steam and warmth of the mug helped soothe her.

"I suppose so. It was worse after Neil died. I thought

the loneliness would crush me back then. But time wore on, and I did my best to stay active and social."

Brittany had been twelve when her grandfather had died. His death had crushed her, too. He'd been the only father figure in her life. She still missed him.

"What about now?"

"It's different. I don't need to be around people as much." Nan ripped open another sugar packet and stirred it into the coffee with shaky fingers.

Brittany's chest squeezed. How much time did she really have left with her grandmother? She lived too far away to visit regularly. Maybe she *should* seriously consider moving Nan out to California with her.

But Mason was right. Nan had lived her entire life in Rendezvous. Dragging her away would be selfish. It would be cruel to take her away from her lifelong home.

She'd find Gabby this afternoon. If she couldn't get Nan to make long-term plans, she could at least hire someone to check on her a few times a week.

But it didn't change the fact she might not have much time left with her grandmother—no matter how many solutions she'd come up with.

"Thanks for meeting me." Mason nodded to Babs O'Rourke in her office at Mountain View Inn. He'd always liked her but tried to avoid her as much as possible. She was a talker. He wasn't. The woman lived for gossip, and he didn't like hearsay, especially when it involved him. But she might hold a key to unlock some of his and Ryder's past.

"Happy to make time for you, sugar." Although she was technically seated in an office chair behind her desk, he wouldn't say she was sitting. Hovering, maybe. She reminded him of a hummingbird. Always in motion. "I was shocked—shocked!—when I ran into your twin. What was it like finding out you have a double? Did you have heart palpitations? Stomach cramps? I don't know what I would do if it happened to me. Probably pass out on the floor. I mean, what if another Babs is out there?"

"There's only one Babs O'Rourke." He couldn't fathom two of her. The world could only handle one. Her bright red hair was locked in place with hairspray, and she wore thick mascara that reminded him of little spider legs.

"I suppose you're right." She let out a throaty laugh. "One of me is plenty. So how did you find out about him— Ryder, is it? Why were you separated? How'd you find each other? I can't believe Gus and Beth never told anyone."

"I'm looking for some of those answers myself. I thought you might be able to help." He inwardly cringed at enlisting the help of the town busybody, but he was desperate.

"Me?" She pressed her palm against her chest, her green eyes widening. "Well, knock me over with a feather. I'm flattered. What can I do?"

"I thought you might know who my father was friends with. Who did he hang around with in high school?"

"Let me think." She grabbed a pen, leaned back and twirled it between her fingers. "John was kind of quiet. Nice kid. Always liked him. When he was younger, he ran around with the Dryden boys. I'm not sure who he hung around with in high school. My daughter Janet was quite a bit younger than him."

Mason's shoulders drooped.

"But I can find out easily enough." She straightened, licked her finger and ripped off a piece of paper from a notepad. "Do you know what year he graduated?"

He told her.

"Good. That'll narrow it down. I'll talk to the gals and get back to you."

Talk to the gals… He curled his lips under. They'd all be talking about him.

But they were probably already talking about him, so what did it matter?

"Thanks. I appreciate it." Preparing to rise, he put his hands on the arms of the chair.

"I see Ada's granddaughter's back in town." She tilted her head. "I remember how you two were inseparable. I haven't seen—what's her name, Brittany?—in a long time. She's prettier than ever. All that sunshine must do her good."

He wasn't touching this conversation. He stood and nodded to her. "Yeah, well, I appreciate you looking into my father's friends."

"I heard she was dating Ryder, and that's how you found out about him."

"You heard wrong." He headed to the door.

"But they drove into town together." She followed him.

"They're not a couple."

"Not anymore? Maybe she's got her sights on you again."

Why did his pulse just take off at a gallop? Ridiculous. He'd been over her for years and nothing was going to change it.

"Call me if you learn anything. And thanks again, Babs." He took long strides down the hall with Babs yammering behind him the entire way.

"Leave it to me, sugar. I'll get back to you lickety-split. Erma Jean's son would have been graduating around the same time, and…"

He rounded the corner and halted. Brittany leaned over the counter to say something and Gabby tossed her head back to laugh.

Why was Brittany here?

Why was she talking to Gabby? He didn't think they knew each other. Were they discussing him? And what was so funny, anyhow?

He marched over to them.

"Hey, Mason." Brittany continued to smile.

"What are you doing here?" He couldn't keep the edge out of his tone.

"Gabby is generously sharing her advice with me."

"Advice? For what?"

"I'm considering hiring a home health aide to come in and help Nan a few times a week. Gabby knows the best people for the job." She turned to Gabby. "Thanks again for your help. I feel so much better knowing there are several good options. Oh, and thanks for the information about the assisted-living facility."

"I'm happy to help. Call me anytime if you have questions or want to talk. I've been down that road with my own grandma and it wasn't easy. Vera Wick is a gem—if you're serious about hiring someone, call her first."

"Well, I'd better get back." Brittany waved.

"I'll walk you out." Mason said goodbye to Gabby and ushered Brittany to the door. Out on the sidewalk, snow swirled. It looked like they'd be getting several inches before morning. He waited until they'd gotten several feet away before turning to her.

"What's this about assisted living?"

Her smile faded. "For future reference. I went with Nan to her doctor's appointment this morning."

"And the doc thinks she needs to be put away?"

"Put away?" She scoffed. "No, he actually thinks she's doing well. She has some short-term memory issues, but he doesn't think it's a problem. If she had dementia, it would be the earliest stage."

"Then why are you worried?"

"I'm trying to plan. That's all."

"I thought we were planning together." He didn't like that she was doing everything on her own—behind his back.

"We are, but I didn't think you'd want me calling you over a few simple details."

He clenched his jaw. She had him there. Stretching his neck from side to side, he tried to calm himself enough to have a rational conversation. "Moving Nan into an old folks' home isn't a simple detail."

"Old folks' home? Being dramatic, aren't you? Don't worry about assisted living." She looked off to the side. "I don't have the authority to make that decision for her."

"What do you mean?"

She made her way to the row of vehicles. "I couldn't put her in an assisted-living facility unless she wanted to go. I can hire home health aides, but if she doesn't want them around, no one can force her to keep them. I don't have power of attorney, and I doubt she'd be willing to go to a lawyer to take care of it, anyhow." She stopped again and faced him. "If she gets worse… I don't know what I'll do."

"You don't need to do anything." Feeling calmer, he raised his palm. He was only inches from her, and although the temperature was cold, heat spread through his body. "You said yourself she's just got a little memory loss."

"How long will it last, though?" She raised herself onto her tippy-toes and slowly lowered down. "I can't be blindsided—I won't be. When I'm back in California, I'll need all the information Gabby just gave me. Because at some point I'm going to get a phone call saying Nan's not eating or she fell or she forgot to turn off the stove." Her shoulders slumped. "I hate feeling so helpless."

Put like that…

He was a mean old snake. Why had he jumped down her throat? She was worried about Nan, trying to relieve her anxieties the only way she knew how, and he was making her feel worse.

Without thinking, he pulled her into his arms. She instantly wrapped hers around his waist and tucked her head under his chin. Exactly the way she used to. Back when she was his.

He couldn't breathe, but he couldn't let go, either. They fit as naturally as they always had. And Babs was right. He and Brittany had been inseparable.

A strong wind blew Brittany's hair up against his face. Her shampoo smelled like coconut. Made him think of the beach and her dancing in the sand, laughing, with her hair streaming behind her and her face tanned by the sun.

All he wanted to do was kiss her. Keep holding her.

It had been three long years since a woman had been in his arms.

Mia's memory cut like ice through him, made him step back quickly. Too quickly.

"We'll figure things out with Nan, don't worry." His voice sounded raspy. He couldn't help it. All he could hear was the pounding of his heart.

"Mason?"

"What?"

"I needed that hug." Her eyes looked suspiciously moist. "Enjoy your time with Ryder tomorrow."

He nodded. Didn't trust himself to speak.

Because he hated to admit it, but he'd needed the hug, too.

He balled his hands into fists as she got into Nan's truck.

His loneliness was betraying him. Betraying Mia.

And it terrified him.

Chapter Eight

The next afternoon Brittany's cell phone rang as she pulled out a tray of sugar cookies from Nan's oven. What if it was the bank? Adrenaline spiked through her body. After plunking the cookie sheet on top of the stove, Brittany lunged for her phone sitting on the counter.

"Hello?" She craned her neck to check on Nan—nodding off in the recliner, as she usually did about this time.

"Brittany?"

"Oh, hi, Mason." The adrenaline surged even harder. *Wonderful.* Her body not only overreacted at the thought of getting her line of credit approved, but at hearing Mason's voice, as well. Having his arms wrapped around her yesterday had really messed with her head.

"I have a favor to ask," he said.

"What's up?" She hadn't heard those words from him in a decade.

"I asked Babs to track down my father's high school friends, and she called earlier with a lead, but the man lives thirty miles away and is leaving tonight to visit his kids for Christmas. And Ryder arrived this morning with his twin girls."

"Okay…" She tried to add up what Mason wanted but drew a blank.

"He says he has something to give us, something that belonged to our dad. We'd like to drive out to see this guy today, but we don't think taking three toddlers is the best move. Eden has an appointment, or she'd watch them. And Gabby thinks Phoebe is getting sick, so she's out, too."

"Do you need me to babysit?"

"Could you?"

"Of course. I love kids." Either he was truly desperate or he was warming up to her. Maybe a little bit of both. Either way, she'd help him out. "Can you bring them over here or should I go out to your ranch?"

"We'll bring them over there." A pause ensued. "They have a lot of energy."

"I've taught countless three-year-olds over the years. I can handle it. In fact, I just baked cookies. They can help me decorate them. And bring outdoor clothes for them— we'll go out to the barn to swing."

"Thanks, I owe you one."

"No, I owe you for all you've done." She did, too. She'd had no idea how much Nan depended on him until she'd spent the week here.

"We'll be over in twenty minutes."

"I'll be waiting." She hung up and stretched from side to side. Three kids? They'd wear her out for sure, but she wouldn't mind one bit. After days of not working, she relished the thought.

She went through each room, trying to think of things that might keep the kids busy. After sliding another batch of cookies into the oven, she taped her secret weapon under the table and prepped a few other items guaranteed to distract toddlers. Then she sat and stared out the front window. The mountains still took her breath away.

But the view couldn't take her mind off Mason's embrace yesterday. After sinking into his arms and enjoying the hug way more than she should have, she'd needed to think. So she'd driven around Rendezvous to get her head straight. But instead of calming her, the anxiety had mounted until she'd finally just parked on a side street in front of an old building. It was an unimaginative rectangular structure with large windows lining the front. A for-sale-by-owner sign hung on the door, and the windows were decaled with High Tech Computer Repairs—Come In For a Quote! From the looks of it, the store had closed for some time.

Why she'd jotted down the number on the sign, she couldn't say. Maybe to compare costs. It would be interesting to know the price of a building here as opposed to the one she was trying to lease in California.

A building here in Rendezvous? Why was she even thinking about it?

Blame it on Mason's strong arms. They'd distracted her, making the California studio a distant thought instead of an urgent need. And the worst part about it was if he would have lowered his head and kissed her...well, she just might have canceled every one of her plans to stay in those arms for good.

She dropped her forehead to her hands. Wanted to bang it once or twice against the window.

A relationship with him was out of the question. All these years later, and it still wouldn't work. Because she was *this close* to the studio, to the dance team, to success.

He didn't want her, anyhow. He needed someone like Mia, someone who would be a partner on the ranch. Actually, he didn't seem to want anyone, which was fine by her.

God, don't let me lose sight of what's important. This—Rendezvous—isn't my life. It's a Christmas vacation. Nothing more.

The slamming of truck doors reached her ears, and a funny zip went down her spine at what she'd gotten herself into.

Energetic preschoolers.

Three of them.

She opened the front door as Noah bounded up the steps in his snow pants and boots. Two girls in matching pink snowsuits chattered behind him. Bringing up the rear were Mason and Ryder. Unlike the girls, they were not wearing identical outfits, but they were stunningly similar nonetheless. One gorgeous Fanning was almost too much to take. But two?

"Miss Bwittany, I got cousins!" Noah kicked off his boots the second he entered the foyer. "That's Harper, and that's Ivy."

The girls stood next to each other on the rug and stared up at her through two pairs of deep blue eyes. Under their purple stocking caps, dark brown hair hung down their backs. They each had a button nose and long eyelashes. They were destined to be beauties.

"Hi, Harper and Ivy!" She plastered on her brightest smile.

"Hey, Brittany." Ryder gave her a brotherly hug. "How's your visit been so far?"

"Really good." She waited for Mason to shut the door. "I can't believe how fast it's going, though. Christmas is, what, five days away?"

Nan came over, beaming. But her expression faltered as she studied Ryder. "Mason?"

"Over here, Nan." Mason stepped forward. "This is the brother I told you about, Ryder."

"There are two of you."

"Yep, we're twins."

"Remember we told you a few days ago?" Brittany helped the girls remove their snow gear. Now that the doctor had told her Nan experienced some short-term memory loss, the forgetful moments didn't seem as sinister as they had when she'd first arrived.

"Oh…" She frowned. "Yes."

"It's a pleasure to meet you, ma'am." Ryder shook her hand. "These are my girls, Ivy and Harper."

"Sweet children." Nan smiled as she studied the girls. "Hello, dears."

"I'm here, too, Nan." Noah strutted to Nan and gave her a hug.

She bent and kissed the top of his head. "Of course you are, Noah."

Ryder's twins continued to stare at Brittany.

"We're going to have fun today," she said to them.

"This is Harper." Ryder put his hands on the shoulders of the girl in the red shirt. "And this is Ivy." He gestured to the girl in green. Then he crouched in front of them. "Remember what we talked about? I'll be back in a couple of hours with Uncle Mason. In the meantime, you mind Miss Brittany, okay?"

"Okay, Daddy!" They both threw their arms around him.

"You have my cell number if you need anything." Mason met her eyes. His gaze was brooding, intense. "And you can always call Bill and Joanna if you have any trouble."

"We'll be fine." She shooed him and Ryder out the door. "Go. Get some answers."

Out on the porch, Mason turned back. The glint in his eyes sent a shiver over her skin. She waited for him to say something, but he must have thought better of it and continued down the steps.

Strange. She closed the door and faced the kids. They stared at her with wide-eyed expectation.

"Let's play a game to get to know each other better." She bounced over to the kitchen table.

"I like games." Noah climbed onto a chair. Harper and Ivy reached for the same chair and started arguing over it. It was a good thing Brittany had dealt with young children extensively over the years. Their attention spans were notoriously short. She always had a bag of tricks up her sleeve.

"This is your special chair, Ivy." Brittany pulled out the one on the end. Ivy gave her sister a triumphant smile as she climbed up.

"And Harper, this is your special chair." She pulled out the one on the other end. Harper stuck her tongue out at Ivy. Then Brittany sat across from Noah. "There. Now everyone is exactly where they're supposed to be."

"What about Nan?" Noah asked.

"Do you want to join us, Nan?" Brittany called.

"Maybe a little later, honey."

"What's the game?" Noah asked. "Do we use a spinner?"

"No spinner. We use a special wand."

"Where's the special wand?" Harper, sitting on her knees on the chair, bounced with enthusiasm.

"It's right here." Brittany pulled the wand out from where she'd taped it under the table earlier. It was a pink pen with a huge—and very soft—faux fur pom-pom on the end. She leaned in with a secretive air. "Do you want to know the rules?"

Ivy blinked through big eyes and nodded.

"Whoever has the wand gets to answer a question.

We take turns. And we listen until it's our turn to speak. How does that sound?"

"Me first!" Noah reached for the wand. But Brittany held it back.

"We're going in order. We'll start with Harper. What is your favorite color?" She handed it to the right, and Harper clutched it with both hands.

"Pink!" Her little cheeks were rosy.

"I love pink, too." Brittany nodded in encouragement. "Go ahead and pass it to Noah. Noah, what's your favorite color?"

"Blue. Like the sky."

"Ooh, nice. The sky is very blue here in the summer, isn't it?"

"Yeah, and I like riding under it on a horse with my daddy. We go all over—up the hills and down to the creek. The sky's real blue."

"I want to ride a horse." Harper's eyes practically glowed.

"It's a lot of fun," Brittany said. "Okay, Ivy's turn."

Noah handed the wand to her. She instantly rubbed it against her chin, closing her eyes. "It's soft, like a bunny."

Brittany's heart flip-flopped at the girl's simple joy. "What's your favorite color, Ivy?"

"Don't you say pink." Harper jutted her lower lip out. "No copying."

"I wasn't going to say pink, Harper." Her little nose tilted up. "I like green."

"Green is very pretty." Brittany gestured for her to hand over the wand. She held it with both hands and looked one by one at the children. "And I like the color aqua."

"Aqua?" Noah's forehead creased. "What's that?"

"It's a very light bluish green. Like the ocean."

"I like aqua, too." Ivy batted her lashes.

"Me, too." Harper bounced on the chair.

"If it's got blue, I like it," Noah conceded.

They continued passing the wand around and answering questions until Brittany sensed they were getting bored. She set the wand on the counter. "Should we go out to the barn and swing for a while?"

"Swing!" Noah yelled.

She ruffled his hair. "What do you say, girls? Want to check out the barn?"

"Yeah!" Harper yelled. She ran after Noah, who was halfway into his snow pants.

Ivy hung back. Brittany bent to talk to her. "You don't have to swing if you don't want to."

"I never been in a barn." Worry lines grew between her eyes.

"I think you'll like it. Do you like kitties?"

"I love kitties." In a flash, her expression brightened.

"Well, Nan has a bunch of fluffy cats out there. We can pet them."

"Really? My mama says we can't have no kitties."

She rose and put her hand on Ivy's shoulder. "You can borrow ours today."

For the next hour, Brittany pushed the three children on the tire swing—they all fit on it at the same time—and let them feed, water and pet the cats to their hearts' delight. She loved every minute of it, even the times they occasionally squabbled.

All three had distinct personalities. Noah had already cast himself in the role of protector. It was cute watching him puff out his chest. Harper wasn't going to be outdone by a boy, and she did whatever he did and seemed to love every minute. Ivy was content to just be with them. A quieter girl, she preferred to sit with the cats while Noah and Harper chased each other through the barn, throwing straw in the air.

When they'd had their fill of fun, they trekked back to the house through the snow.

"I like snow." Ivy bent to scoop some into her gloved hands. "We don't get it where we live. Look at how sparkly it is."

"I like it, too, Ivy." Harper clomped over and kissed Ivy on the cheek. "This is fun."

The sweet gesture pulled at Brittany's heart. What precious little girls.

"Are we having cookies now, Miss Bwittany?" Noah reached up to hold her hand through his mittens.

"Yes, we are. And you guys get to help decorate them."

"We do?"

"Yes."

"Yay!" They all shrieked and jumped and, laughing, fell into the snow.

"Look, I'm making a snow angel." Noah waved his arms and legs. The girls imitated him. They stood up and admired their work, then they were off again.

As the children ran ahead of her, Brittany's feet refused to move. It was if an air horn blasted in her brain.

She wanted kids.

Wanted to be a mother.

She ached to have a husband, a home and children to raise.

Her cell phone rang. She fumbled to see who it was. Hopefully, Mason and Ryder weren't worried about the kids.

The bank. Her heart jumped to her throat and her palms grew clammy.

"Hello?" She climbed the steps to the back porch and let the kids inside.

"I'm sorry I missed your call the other day, Miss Green. We're still waiting on information before we'll have an answer on your line of credit. I didn't want you to think we forgot about you. Expect a call early next week."

"Thank you." She hung up, sliding the phone back into her pocket.

The studio beckoned. If the bank came through, she'd be able to add hardwood floors and mirrors to the rooms in the building she planned on leasing, outfit a small waiting area for the parents, hire more instructors, offer more classes and quit her extra jobs.

She'd finally have made it—she'd finally be successful.

She entered the back door.

"Can you help me get my boot off, Miss Brittany?" Ivy lay on the floor with one leg in the air.

"Of course." She pulled off the boot and unzipped the girl's coat. The building here in town popped into her mind, but she dismissed it. Rendezvous was tiny. It would never have enough serious dancers to put a team together.

But then again…

Rendezvous might not have the numbers for an elite dance team, but it had its own charms. Nan. Mason. Noah.

Her mother's voice rang through her mind. *Don't throw away your dreams for a middle-of-nowhere town.*

Don't worry, Mom. She lined up the boots on the rug. *It was only a fantasy.*

He didn't have a good feeling about this. Mason carried a stack of pizza boxes into his kitchen that night. Trying to be proactive about introducing his in-laws to Ryder, he'd invited Bill, Joanna and Eden over for supper, with Ryder's blessing. But earlier, when he and Ryder had picked up the kids, his brother had invited Nan and Brittany to join them, too.

Naturally, the kids had grabbed Brittany's hands and pleaded with her to come until, laughing, she'd agreed. Nan had seemed pleased, as well.

He couldn't un-invite them. But having Brittany and his in-laws together was bound to be uncomfortable.

"Does anyone want pop?" He set the pizzas on the counter.

"Me, me, me!" the three kids yelled.

"I'll handle it." Ryder chuckled. "I'll get them something without caffeine."

"Good plan."

"Is it okay if we come in?" Bill's voice carried from the foyer.

"Come on in." Mason pivoted and went down the hall to greet them. Joanna and Eden were taking off their coats.

Bill held up a covered casserole dish. "Joanna's bacon cheeseburger dip."

"How did you know I was hungry for it?" He kissed his mother-in-law's cheek.

"It's your favorite." She flushed and handed him a bag of tortilla chips.

"Your appointment go okay?" Mason asked Eden.

"It was fine. No cavities." She flashed her white teeth. "Sorry I couldn't watch Noah and the girls for you."

"Don't apologize. You have a life, too."

He didn't miss her slight frown. Had he said something wrong?

"Why don't you go back to the kitchen. I'll introduce you to Ryder." He waited until they were halfway down the hall before adding, "Nan and Brittany will be here soon."

Bill shot him a backward glance full of suspicion. Mason busied himself hanging up the coats. He'd just keep the conversation flowing and hope for the best.

"Grandpa!" Noah ran from the living room. "I got cousins!"

"That's what I hear, Spurs. Where are these young ladies?" Bill let Noah take him by the hand to the living room. Mason followed them.

"That's Harper, and that's Ivy." He pointed to the girls, both lying on their tummies with their chins propped on their hands and their feet kicking behind them as they watched a Christmas cartoon. At the introduction, they rolled over and stood. Ivy hung back while Harper went up to Bill.

"Well, I'll be." Bill had his happy grandpa voice on. "You have the purdiest cousins I ever did see, Spurs."

Both girls giggled.

"What were your names again? Curly and Joe?" He pointed to them.

"No, silly! I'm Harper." The little girl jammed her thumb into her chest.

"I'm Ivy." She stared up through shy eyes.

"Delighted to meet you." He shook their hands. They giggled again.

Mason cleared his throat. "And this is Ryder." He clapped his hand on Ryder's shoulder.

Bill's face went blank and Joanna blinked again and again. Eden had paled.

"I knew it was true…but seeing you together…it's incredible." Joanna rushed forward with arms wide-open and hugged Ryder. "You really are twins."

"Good to meet you." Bill had recovered and shook Ryder's hand. "You've got cute kids."

"Thank you. It's a pleasure to meet you, too, sir."

"Oh, and this is my sister-in-law, Eden." Mason nodded to her. "I don't know what I'd do without her. She takes care of Noah for me while I'm working."

"Good to meet you, Eden." Ryder shook her hand.

"You, too."

Noise from the front porch caught his attention. "That must be Nan. I'll be right back."

Mason jogged to the entrance and let them inside. After helping Nan remove her coat, he pointed her to the living room.

Brittany caught his arm. Questions swam in her blue eyes. He had the worst urge to hold her again. Instead, he stiffened.

"Are you sure you want us here?" she asked.

What was he supposed to say? *No, but my brother insisted and the kids acted like you're Mary Poppins and I didn't want to look like the mean guy.*

"Yes." He hung Nan's coat up. Brittany was twitching around on her feet as she nibbled her lower lip. He sighed. "Come on, I'll introduce you."

His in-laws were cordial to Brittany, but Mason didn't miss the slight narrowing of Bill's eyes. At least Eden made an effort to talk to her.

"Let's eat." Mason extended his arm to the kitchen.

Everyone got a plate of food and found a place to sit, either at the table or counter.

"You're Joanie's daughter, aren't you?" Bill asked Brittany.

"I am."

"Staying in these parts long?"

"Just until after Christmas." She took another bite of her slice of pepperoni. "Did you know my mother well?"

"No." He grunted. "I knew of her. She was younger than me. Flighty thing."

"Bill!" Joanna whispered, shocked.

"What?" He acted innocent.

Mason decided it was time to change the subject. "Ryder and I met with a friend of our dad's today, Jake Simmons."

"His name doesn't ring a bell," Joanna said. "How did it go?"

"Not as well as I'd hoped. He's a nice man, but he lost touch with our dad after high school. He didn't have any clues to share about why we were separated."

"He *did* give us a shoebox he'd kept," Ryder said. "There were some pictures of our dad and Jake, ticket stubs from movies and concerts and a small book filled with rodeo stats they recorded every summer. Who knew John Fanning was such a bull-riding buff? Apparently he never got on one himself, though. Jake said John loved crunching numbers. Accounting is my line of work. Uncanny, isn't it? Although, being out here makes me miss ranching."

"You used to ranch? I took you for a city boy." Bill shifted to face Ryder.

"Grew up on a sheep ranch in Montana. All that bare, lonely land—I never thought I'd miss it. But being around people all the time isn't easy."

"You can say that again." Bill chuckled.

"I like being around people." Brittany looked as if she couldn't believe the words had come out of her mouth.

"Good thing you're in California, then," Bill said.

"Yes, it is," she said quietly.

Mason watched her. A melancholy air had fallen over her, and, against his will, he wanted to cheer her up, the way he used to. She leaned over and whispered something to Nan. Nan nodded, and Brittany handed her a napkin.

"How long you in town, then, Ryder?" Bill asked.

"A week. We're leaving next Saturday."

Eden frowned. "The girls won't see their mother for Christmas?"

"No, she's on location." Ryder's face hardened.

"On location?" Joanna seemed confused.

"She's an actress." His face grew red.

"Oh, anyone we'd know?" Joanna asked.

"Lily Haviland."

"You're married to Lily Haviland?" Eden's jaw scraped the floor. "She's famous."

"Don't I know it," he said, almost under his breath.

"Mom, she's the one who plays Rain on *Courtroom Crimes* and was in that romantic comedy we saw in the theater last summer."

"Oh, right, the striking brunette with those piercing eyes." Joanna opened her hands, palms outward. "She's charismatic."

"She's a good actress." Ryder kept his tone neutral. "We've recently divorced."

"Oh." An awkward silence fell over the room.

"I signed the papers last month." His shoulders slumped.

"Well, we're glad you're spending Christmas here, with family." Brittany gave Ryder a sympathetic smile as she stood and threw away her paper plate.

The way she seamlessly shifted the conversation to make Ryder comfortable touched Mason's heart. He'd forgotten how kind she could be. Or maybe over the years he'd convinced himself she had no good qualities.

He'd been wrong. She had plenty of good qualities.

"I'm done, Daddy." Ivy held up her paper plate. It had half a slice of pizza on it.

"Can you eat two more bites, pumpkin?"

"I'm full." She patted her tummy.

"I'm full, too." Harper's plate held the crust of her slice.

"Not me. I'm still hungry." Noah got up to get another piece.

"Let me help you." Eden scrunched her nose as she smiled at Noah. She set a small piece of pizza on his plate.

He blew her a kiss. "Thanks, Auntie Eden. I love you."

"I love you, too. And we're going to have fun tomorrow. It's Christmas Fest."

"Christmas Fest!" He turned to the twins. "We're gonna skate and see Santa and feed reindeer and have hot cocoa and…"

"Christmas Fest?" Ryder rubbed his chin. "Sounds fun. Brittany, you should come with us."

"Oh, no." She gave him a tight smile. "I can't."

Mason knew she was lying, and although he should have been glad she declined, he couldn't help wishing she'd said yes.

Less than a week. Just keep it together until after Christmas. Remember your promise? Mia was it for you. Period. Brittany will leave and you'll forget about her.

But something told him she wouldn't be so easy to forget.

Chapter Nine

"Why don't you stroll around and have some fun." Lois Dern nudged her. Brittany had been sitting at the end of the table for over an hour. Nan sat between Lois and Gretchen Sable, behind the display at the Christmas Fest bake sale located in the rec center. Craft stations and displays of toy trains filled the rest of the space. Lois leaned in. "Christmas Fest is for you young ones. Get out there and go skating."

"I'm happy here, Lois."

Gretchen had left a message on the machine last night to remind Nan they were taking a shift selling sweets. Nan had forgotten about it, but she'd wanted to go, so Brittany had driven her here and stayed.

Brittany enjoyed listening to their conversation. Gretchen had spent ten minutes fussing over the way some lady named Betsy from church had taken it upon herself to change the meeting place of the women's group. And Lois was worried her great-grandchild was going to terrorize her Miniature Schnauzer at Christmas dinner next week. Nan had even added to the conversation here and there. They all clearly cared about each other.

"You're not going to round up a hunky cowboy sitting

here." Lois fluffed her short white curls. "This is prime hunting ground for finding a fella."

"She might not want a fella, Lois. She's a career gal." Gretchen peered around Nan to Brittany. Brittany had never been referred to as a *career gal* before, but she supposed it was true. Working three jobs didn't exactly feel like a career, though. "You should at least go skating even if you're not looking for a boyfriend. We're blessed the weather cooperated this year."

"A pretty thing like her?" Lois said. "She should be able to snatch one of these boys right up. Misty Sandpiper's got nothing on Nan's granddaughter."

"That's not charitable, Lois." Gretchen shook her head.

"Well, I guess I'm not charitable, then, am I?" The ladies proceeded to engage in a very intense stare-off.

"If Judd were here, I'd insist he take you skating, Brittany." Gretchen wiggled her shoulders as her mouth drew into a thin line. She turned to Lois. "Misty has been sniffing around him again."

Who in the world was Judd? And she really wanted to catch a glimpse of this Misty Sandpiper.

"Miss Bwittany!" Noah dragged Mason by the hand over to their table. Ryder, the twins and Eden weren't far behind.

"Hey, guys, are you having fun?" Brittany stood to greet them all. Her heart hammered as she tried not to stare at Mason. The girls came over and hugged her. All three of the kids began talking at once, and she laughed. "One at a time, sillies!"

Harper held up a small bag of gumdrops, and Ivy raved about feeding the reindeer. Noah asked her which cupcake on the table was the best. She pointed him to the triple chocolate one.

"Daddy, can I have a cupcake?" He tugged on Mason's

coat. Mason met her eyes and a flash of awareness rippled over her skin. The man got more handsome every time she saw him.

"So the rumors are true." Lois stood and smiled at Mason. "You've got a twin."

"I do. This is my brother, Ryder. Ryder, this is Mrs. Dern and Mrs. Sable, and you remember Nan."

Ryder said hello to them all. They chitchatted for a few minutes while the kids picked out cupcakes.

"We're going skating." Noah slipped his little hand in Brittany's. "I want you to come with us."

"Me, too!" Harper jumped up, clapping her hands.

"Me, too!" Ivy said.

"Go on, honey." Lois waved her away.

"I should get Nan home soon." She didn't want to insert herself into Mason's day.

"Ada's fine. We're getting a bite to eat after the next shift arrives, and afterward we'll take her home."

"I don't know." Brittany glanced at Nan. "I think I'll stay with you."

"Don't worry about me." Nan looked content. And she was in good hands. "Go with Mason."

Did she even have a choice at this point?

"Guess you're skating with us." Mason's eyes gleamed. Was he happy? Mad? Once upon a time, she'd known him, been able to read him. But now…she wasn't sure what went on behind those caramel-brown depths.

"Yay!" Noah yelled.

"Let's go rent skates." Ryder grabbed a few napkins to clean up the girls.

Harper held her arms up for Eden to carry her, and Eden smiled radiantly as she obliged. Mason's sister-in-law was a natural with children. She loved them and they loved her. With her long brown hair and dark brown eyes, she was very pretty and very quiet. Mason seemed close to her.

Why wouldn't he be close to her? The woman babysat his child.

Brittany shrugged her arms into her winter coat with a touch too much force. Had he and Eden ever had a romantic connection?

What did she care about Mason's romantic life? It was none of her business. After all, she was a career gal. Not ranch wife material.

Ryder carried Ivy, and Mason hauled Noah into his arms.

Everyone held a child but her. She might as well wear a sign with Single and Childless on it. But Eden wasn't married, either. She didn't have kids. Brittany glanced her way. Why hadn't *she* rounded up one of the cowboys Lois had mentioned?

What is your problem, Brit? You are a career gal. You don't want to be a ranch wife. None of this bothered you before yesterday.

As they neared the door, the crowd pushed her closer to Mason.

"I didn't peg you for the ice-skating type." She looked up at him, trying to keep her tone teasing.

"There are a lot of things you don't know about me, Brittany." They reached the exit. He waited for her to go through it.

"You're right." There were ten years of things she didn't know about him. And right now she wanted those years back. Wanted to know more.

Outside, she stared in wonder. Rendezvous was decked out for the holidays. It was the first time she'd ever been in such a winter wonderland at Christmastime. Centennial Street was closed to traffic. Street vendors sold hot chocolate, barbecue sandwiches, fries and funnel cakes. Signs pointed to the city park for ice-skating, live reindeer and sleigh rides.

"This is amazing!" She stuck her hat on her head and put on her gloves. "Okay, fill me in. What else don't I know about you? What do you do for fun?"

He seemed surprised and at a loss for words. Then he forged ahead. "I don't have much time for fun."

"Me neither." She took in the families strolling around town, the folks on horseback, the teenagers throwing snow at each other. "But we used to, didn't we? Every summer was an adventure."

"I suppose you're right." His gaze was riveted on her.

"Let's have a good time. For one afternoon, at least."

She didn't care if he argued or wanted to play the who-has-less-time-for-fun game. She might never have another Christmas like this—out in the snow at a festival with an old friend, a new friend and three cute kids. She might as well enjoy it.

But as she glanced up at him, she knew she was fooling herself if she thought this was just a Christmas memory waiting to be made. The more time she spent with Mason and Noah, the more time she wanted to spend with them.

Last night, she'd felt out of place, so she'd spent time observing him. There was tension between him and his in-laws, but she didn't know why. They were all close— it was obvious—but something wasn't right.

What she'd noticed the most, though, was the constant sadness underneath Mason's handsome, kind exterior. He tried to hide it—in fact, he hid it well—but it was there. How she wanted to wrap him in her arms and tell him he didn't have to be sad.

But how could she say it when it wasn't true?

He'd lost his wife. The sadness would likely always be there.

They rounded the corner and the skating rink came into view.

Who could compete with the beautiful, caring wife he'd lost? It wasn't as if she wanted to. She was going back to California in less than a week. It was what she wanted.

Wasn't it?

What did she really want out of life?

"Come on," Ryder called back to them. "I see the line for the skate rental."

Spending all this time with Brittany—having *fun* with her—was a big mistake. Because it only reminded him of old times.

The skating rink brought him back to a different old time, however—one with his wife. Ever since he'd laced up, he'd been fighting off memories of Mia. They'd ice-skated at Christmas Fest on more than one occasion. She'd clung to him, laughing, admiring him, and he hadn't realized how special it had made him feel until she was gone.

Focus on your son.

Mason held one of Noah's hands and Brittany held the other as they skated around the edge of the outdoor rink. Ryder and Harper were skating toward the center, while Eden and Ivy hugged the railing as they made their way around.

"Faster, Daddy!" Noah's skates barely touched the ice. He'd been stumbling so often, Mason had gotten used to keeping the kid upright.

"This is fast enough, buckaroo." He was glad Noah separated him from Brittany. He didn't want to be near her right now. Not with Mia's memories pummeling his heart.

"You're pretty good at this." Brittany shot Mason a grin. "You must have some practice on skates."

"It's not my first time at Christmas Fest." He noticed Brittany was as graceful ice-skating as she was at everything else. Her life as a dancer had prepared her well.

"Is this something you and your wife used to do?" Her question held no undercurrents, but he didn't want to respond. If he did, he might start talking and not be able to stop, and then where would he be?

He had the feeling it wouldn't take much for him to snap. The best-case scenario if that happened would be him ranting about how unfair it was Mia had died. The worst-case scenario? He'd have a complete emotional breakdown in front of the entire town.

He had to stay strong.

"Yes, we did." His tone left no room for further discussion. Emotion tightened his throat, and though skating wasn't taxing for him, he found it difficult to breathe.

"Is this hard for you?" She took the turn smoothly.

He swallowed the emotion jamming his throat and gave her a sidelong glance. Her brilliant blue eyes held curiosity and sympathy. Against his better judgment, he nodded.

"Why don't you take a break and let Noah and I go by ourselves for a few minutes?"

He didn't bother protesting. He did need a break.

"Come on, Noah. We'll drop your daddy off at the bench."

"But I like skating with both of you." His face screwed into a pout.

"I'll go fast," she said. "Maybe your daddy will take some pictures of you."

"Will you, Daddy?" He brightened. "Take a picture of me going real fast!"

"You got it." Mason could barely get out the words. Why was he choked up here of all places? He let go of Noah's hand. "I'll be right over there if you need me." He skated away before he could change his mind.

Finding an empty spot on a bench, he tried to calm the turmoil in his heart.

This was supposed to be a fun day for Noah. Something enjoyable to do with Ryder and the twins. A way to get in the Christmas spirit. It was *not* supposed to trigger all the grief bottled inside him.

And it definitely wasn't supposed to include Brittany.

But he was sure glad she'd joined them.

For some reason, he couldn't imagine her not being here. His gaze found her in the crowd. She held both Noah's hands in hers as she easily skated backward. They'd gravitated toward the center of the rink, and her animated face had captivated his son. The boy beamed at her. Mason could hear his giggles all the way over here.

She glided effortlessly. All that long blond hair swayed under her stocking cap. Her face glowed as she talked to Noah, and his son was equally absorbed in their discussion.

Mason fumbled in his pocket and slid out his phone. He rarely took pictures. It wasn't that he didn't want to; he just never thought of taking them. And this expression— this moment—Mason wanted to capture, because the pure joy on his little boy's face needed to be preserved forever.

He took several pictures, trying to avoid getting Brittany in the shot, but not always succeeding. Then he snapped photos of Ryder and Harper, of Eden and Ivy, and when he'd finished, he slid the phone back in his pocket to sit with his thoughts.

He hadn't realized how hard it would be to come here without Mia. He hadn't been here since she'd died. Last year a snowstorm had canceled the outdoor events, and the previous year, Noah had been too young to come.

"Noah, skate with us!" Harper yelled, waving.

Brittany crouched to talk to Noah. His son nodded, then held her hand as they skated to Ryder and Harper. Seconds later, Brittany stood in front of him.

"Come on." She held out her hand. "You must be cold."

Part of him wanted to take it and skate with her. The other part couldn't handle it.

He took her hand and yanked her down to sit next to him. She let out a shriek.

"You scared me! I thought I was going to fall." She smiled, stretched out her legs, pointed each skate, then tucked them under the bench. "Did you get some pictures?"

"I did." His throat sounded and felt like an old dirt road. "Thanks for taking him around."

"It was fun. He's such a sweet little boy." Her tone sounded wistful.

Hmm…if he wasn't mistaken, she really liked his son.

"Mason?"

"Yeah."

"What was Mia like?" She shifted to see him better.

Had the wind been knocked out of him? He closed his eyes, surprised at how intense his body was reacting to a simple question. How could he answer it?

Mia was the calm after a storm, light on morning dewdrops, a safe place to land.

Man, the backs of his eyes stung.

"She was special." He choked on the words.

Brittany put her arm around his shoulders and leaned her cheek against his arm. "I'm sorry she died.

I'm sorry you lost her. I'm sorry you have to raise Noah without her."

Trying to suppress tears, he blinked again and again, and finally wiped his eyes with the back of his hand.

"Me, too." He turned to her then and nodded.

"Do you talk about her much?" The compassion in her eyes pulled him in.

"No."

"You can, you know. It's okay. It might help."

"It won't. She's gone. Talking won't bring her back."

"I know. It might preserve her for you, though." She averted her gaze. Her feet began sliding back and forth under the bench. "When I was in college, I was determined to forget you. Every time I thought of you, my heart hurt so bad, I thought putting it into a meat grinder would be easier. My roommate, Ally, got mad at me one day and told me she didn't know what my problem was, but whatever I was doing wasn't working. Then she threw a pillow at my head. And I hurled it right back at hers. We called a truce and sat side by side with our knees tucked to our chests as we ate cheese puffs. I started telling her about meeting you at the tire swing each summer. The way we'd splash in the creek. How you taught me how to ride a horse. The dances I choreographed and dragged you into. And slowly, it didn't hurt as much."

"You missed me?" He'd always assumed she'd forgotten about him the instant she left Rendezvous. That her college days had been so fun, she hadn't thought about him one bit.

"What kind of question is that?" She nudged him with her elbow. "Of course I missed you. You were my best friend. I… I cared about you very much. I can't tell you how many letters I wrote to you."

"I never got any."

"You wouldn't have. I crumpled them up and threw them in the trash."

"Why?"

"You know why."

He did. In one week, he'd practically forgotten about his decade-long grudge.

How long would it take before he forgot Mia, too?

Brittany shrugged. "I'm just saying talking about the good times hurts less than trying to forget them."

"I'm not trying to forget. I'm trying to hold on to them." The words she'd said made sense, but he didn't trust the concept. Maybe he was lying to himself.

"Then talk about them, write them down, remember them."

"It's too hard." He ducked his chin.

"You're the toughest cowboy I know. Why not start small. How did you propose to her?"

"You really want to do this?" He searched her expression for any hint of insincerity. He saw nothing but gentleness. And the weird thing? He ached to talk about Mia.

"Yeah, I do."

"I proposed to her on a mild day in June. She and I went horseback riding on her family's ranch. They have a neat little picnic spot on the north end of the property. It's on the river, real close to the mountains. I was a nervous wreck. I'd patted my pocket no less than fifty times after dismounting. Mia kept asking me if something was wrong. I had it all planned—I was going to guide her to the river, pretend to see a big trout, get on my knee and propose."

He shook his head. Brittany's smile distracted him momentarily.

"Go on." She made a rolling gesture with her hand. "What went wrong?"

"The riverbank was slick, and my boot sunk into it. Mia was grabbing my shoulder, yelling for me not to fall in, and I lost my balance. Fell backward onto my behind."

She chuckled.

"It worked out better that way," he said. "I tugged her onto my lap and begged her to marry me."

"I'm sure it didn't take much begging," she said softly.

"It didn't."

The rest of that day replayed in his mind, and he relaxed. It had been one of the best days of his life. For the first time in ages, he could picture Mia exactly the way she'd looked that day.

"Thank you." He shifted to face Brittany.

"Daddy! Daddy!" Noah called from the ice. "Watch this!"

Eden lightly held his hand as he attempted to skate, then she let go, and he skated a few steps on his own before she grabbed hold of him again. Laughing, they made their way over to the bench.

"You did it! You skated by yourself." Mason wrapped Noah into a big hug. "Good job."

"I did!"

Ryder was slowly skating toward them. He held Harper's hand, and Harper held Ivy's hand. He was talking on his cell phone, and from the look on his face, he wasn't happy.

"Relocate? It's out of the country. No way. I can't believe you would be this selfish." The vein in Ryder's forehead throbbed. "I've got to go." He hung up the phone.

"I'd be happy to take the girls for a hot cocoa if you get another phone call." Eden gave him a pointed glare. The twins were holding each other's hands tightly and seemed ready to cry.

His mouth thinned to a fine line. "This doesn't concern you."

Hurt flashed in Eden's eyes before she turned away.

"Hot cocoas are a great idea." Brittany stood and addressed the children. "I want extra marshmallows in mine."

"Me, too!" All three joined in the chorus.

Once again, she'd diffused a tense situation. Mason was beginning to think it wouldn't be so bad for Brittany to be around for good.

But who was he kidding? There wasn't anything here to make her stay.

Today had raised a lot of questions.

A little after nine o'clock that evening, Brittany tapped her cell phone against her leg. She and Nan had eaten barbecue sandwiches they'd brought home from Christmas Fest for dinner while watching *A Charlie Brown Christmas* on television. They'd talked about Nan's childhood and how much she'd enjoyed moving into this house as a bride with Brittany's grandpa. Nan went into great detail about how they scraped together the money to buy furniture. Half an hour ago, Nan had yawned and promptly went to bed.

Being here all week had painted a more complete picture of Nan's health than Brittany could've previously envisioned. Sure, the woman had an odd reluctance to shower. She forgot what she was doing before she left a room. She napped her way through the day. But she also ate the meals Brittany placed in front of her, and she remembered her past in vivid detail.

Time was growing short. Christmas Eve was Tuesday—only three days away—and Brittany was going back to California the day after Christmas. She needed to make decisions about Nan's future soon. Would Nan allow an aide to come over a few times a week? What if her health got worse? What was she going to do about the whole power of attorney thing?

Maybe Lois would have some insight.

She padded to the kitchen and found Nan's address book. Flipping through the pages, she stopped at the *D*s and typed in Lois's number before she could talk herself out of it.

"Dern residence. Lois speaking."

"Hi, Lois, it's Brittany."

"Oh, hi, darlin'. It sure was good to see you today. What can I help you with? Say, Ada's okay, isn't she?"

"Yes, she is. She went to bed a little while ago. I'm hoping you could give me some advice."

"You came to the right place, hon." She laughed.

"I'm not sure what to do about Nan."

"Do about her? I'm not following you."

Brittany told her about her concerns with Nan's hygiene, eating habits and forgetfulness. "The doctor isn't concerned, but I'm not sure. I don't feel right leaving her like this."

"She's getting old. Happens to the best of us. Her life isn't perfect, and it doesn't need to be. What are you wanting to do?"

"I thought I could hire a home health aide to come in a few days a week to help out. Or we could tour the assisted-living facilities in the area. She could always come to California and live with me."

"How does she feel about those options?"

"I don't know." Brittany rubbed her chin, wishing this was easier.

"I'll come by more often. I can throw out her leftovers from now on. It probably wouldn't hurt to hire someone to come over and help her shower. Mason checks on her daily. I stop by once a week. Gretchen stops by, too."

Lois had a point. People watched out for Nan. Maybe living here by herself wasn't the nightmare waiting to happen Brittany had been imagining.

"I guess I could get her an emergency button in case she fell. I'm not sure what to do about her bills, though."

"Isn't she paying them?"

"She is. For now. But I worry it will get to a point where she'll forget them."

"Why not get them all set up for auto-pay through her bank account?"

She hadn't thought of that. "That's a great idea. I'll run it by her. Maybe I could help her set it up before I leave. I hope she'll let me. She did not like me asking about her having a power of attorney at all."

"My son is mine, but he lives in a neighboring town. If Ada was to name someone power of attorney, Mason would be a good option."

"Mason? Why?" Didn't Lois think she was qualified for the task?

"He lives here, honey. It will be awfully difficult for you to see to Nan's affairs way down in California."

Another good point.

"If you want to have a home health aide come in, you should talk to Vera Wick at church. She's certified."

That was two recommendations for Vera—she sounded like the perfect solution.

Lois continued. "And you might want to play up to your grandmother's charitable side."

"What do you mean?"

"Make her think she'd be doing Vera the favor. Vera won't mind." Lois coughed. "Will you promise me one thing? Tell me you'll talk to your grandma before making any decisions. This is her life. She's doing pretty well for her age. Respect that."

"I will, Lois. Thank you." After a few more minutes, she hung up. Lois was right. Nan deserved the respect of being asked what she wanted. It wasn't Brittany's call to completely overhaul her life. But she still didn't know what the best option was, and until she had more clarity, she didn't want to initiate the conversation.

So far her visit had been full of contradictions, ups and downs, and surprises. She stretched out her back, then sat on the floor and began stretching each leg. The easing of the tight muscles relaxed her. Her ankles were sore. She frowned—must be from ice-skating.

Skating with Mason and Noah had been fun at first. And then things had changed.

When Mason opened up to her about how he proposed to Mia, she'd felt as if she were right there. The look on his face as he'd talked had made the hair on her arms rise. He'd looked so happy. In love. Young—like the Mason she'd grown up with.

Then he'd mentioned tugging Mia onto his lap, and Brittany became aware of loss. His loss.

And her own.

Mason was the only man she'd ever loved. And another woman had gotten his love. All of it.

The teasing, the butterflies, the dates, the proposal. The wedding, the mundane chores, the big ranch house and the ranch to go with it.

The baby.

The family.

Mia had gotten it all, and she would never begrudge her that.

But Brittany mourned for the things she didn't have, the things she might never have.

Tears welled in her eyes.

Poor Mia. The woman had it all and lost it. It didn't seem right her life had been cut short.

Brittany had gotten a glimpse of what the loss had done to Mason.

It had hollowed him out. And all she wanted to do was make him whole again.

She sniffled and grabbed a tissue. For the first time in years, she wanted to remember her special times with Mason. In fact, she wanted to recall every moment she'd spent with him. She'd avoided thinking about him out of guilt and, in the process, lost out on the blessings of those summer days.

Crossing over to the shelves where Nan kept old photo albums and books, she wiped her tears and selected a stack of albums. What better place to start than here?

Chapter Ten

"I feel like I'm looking at pictures of myself." Ryder held up a photo from when Mason was in elementary school. "I think I had this same shirt."

Mason laughed. "You had good taste, man."

It was past ten on Saturday night. All three kids had conked out early. He and Ryder had been trading childhood stories ever since tucking them in. On his knees, Mason dug through the final box of old documents he'd gotten from the attic, and Ryder sat nearby with a pile of photos on his lap.

"It's funny how time changes you." Ryder set the picture down. "In the summer, Granddad and I used to drive for what felt like a million miles to the middle of nowhere to check on the sheep herders and drop off supplies. I don't know how they did it. Loneliest places you'd ever see. It's funny, but I catch myself thinking about their trailers every so often. I wouldn't mind spending a few weeks in one of them. Nobody breathing down my neck, no drama. Escape from it all, you know?"

"I get it." He slid a paper out from an envelope and scanned the contents. Nothing important. "My favorite part of the day is when I saddle up before the sun rises. It's just me and Bolt, the ranch hands and a few herding dogs. No one needs to have a conversation. We all know what to do. It's the closest thing to peace I've found since..." He and Ryder had been growing close, sharing their pasts, but neither had volunteered a word about their wives.

Had he been wrong to confide in Brittany earlier? After he'd told her about proposing to Mia, he'd expected to berate himself, but he hadn't. Because talking about the good times had left him feeling a tiny bit lighter. And he'd do anything to throw off the heaviness he'd carried since her death. Maybe he should open up more to his brother.

"It's been hard since Mia died." There. He'd said it.

"How did she die?"

"Cancer. Six months after Noah was born." He was getting emotional. *Don't cry.* Taking a deep breath, he continued. "We found out while she was pregnant. Treatment would have hurt the baby, so she refused, and afterward, it was too late."

"I'm sorry." Ryder got up and put his hand on his shoulder. And Mason felt it then—the connection to this man whom he resembled so closely. He rose and pulled him in for a hug.

Ryder clutched him tightly, then clapped him on the back and sat down again.

"You spent a lot of time with your grandfather, huh?" Mason swallowed twice in an effort to ease his emotions.

"I did. He had high expectations and not much affection. I learned a lot from him, though. I'm grateful he raised me as a cowboy."

"Yeah, and you're a big city boy now, aren't you?" he teased, slowly feeling normal again. "Are you sure there's any cowboy left? I can tell you wear fancy suits to work and hold meetings in conference rooms. You

probably even have business lunches. My own brother…
gone corporate."

"As a matter of fact, I do wear fancy suits and I might
even let you borrow one sometime. I hate the meetings.
They are the most pointless things on earth. Nothing gets
done. Now business lunches on the other hand…yeah, I
like them."

"Why?" Mason glanced up from the wad of envelopes
he'd grabbed.

"The food. My clients have expensive tastes, and I like
a good meal." He patted his stomach.

"You have a point."

They sat in easy silence as Mason skimmed letters
and Ryder studied the pictures.

"I've been thinking about our visit to Dad's friend yesterday." Ryder glanced at him.

"Oh yeah?"

"All this time, and the guy knew our dad had gotten a
degree and a job in finance—but I never knew it."

"Me neither." He wasn't sure where Ryder was going
with this.

"It makes me feel good I have a connection with him—
that both of us were drawn to finance."

Something Mason didn't have. He'd never been a fan
of keeping the ranch's books.

"But I also wonder what we have in common with
our mom. No one seems to know what she was like. My
grandparents never talked about her. I don't have ties to
my hometown anymore. Who knew her? Someone had
to have been close to Lisa Fanning."

"I do have a picture." Mason got to his feet. One mea-
sly photograph, which was strange in itself. Ma and Pops
had to have met her at some point.

"I don't have any," Ryder said. "I remember seeing

some when I was real little, but when I was in grade school, our basement flooded and destroyed the photos with it. I wish I would have snuck a few up to my room. I tried once. Granddad found them and yelled at me to leave the pictures alone. He took them with him."

Mason frowned. Granddad sounded harsh. But losing his daughter... Mason conceded grief made people act out of character sometimes. He of all people knew it firsthand. How many times had he been harsh with Bill or Joanna? Even Eden had gotten the brunt of his bad mood at times.

"Can I see it?" Ryder asked.

"Of course. I'll go get it. Be right back." He went to the staircase. Why wouldn't Ma and Pops have accepted their son's wife? If his dad had really wanted to ranch, a wife wouldn't have stopped him. Pops blaming her didn't make much sense. But maybe he hadn't approved of her because she was manipulative. Or mean.

He rummaged through his bedside drawer until he found the picture. Looking into his mother's smiling face, he didn't believe she was a bad person.

He brought it downstairs and handed it to Ryder.

"They're together." Ryder's voice held a touch of awe. "They look happy, don't they?"

"Yeah, they do."

He stared over Ryder's shoulder to study the picture. John had his arms around Lisa, and she leaned with her back to his chest. She was gazing sideways up at him. Her blond hair was permed, and her face had delicate features.

"We look like our dad." Ryder tapped John's image. "But I think we have her eyes."

Mason squinted. "I think you're right."

"Well, they were in love, at least." Ryder sounded discouraged. "And we have proof our parents existed."

"We'll keep looking for answers. Maybe we could track down friends of theirs from college. We could take a road trip to Colorado sometime."

He looked pensive. "Maybe we'll never know much about them or why our grandparents separated us."

"I don't know if I can accept that."

"When I think of Lily and I—" he shook his head "—I don't know. We were happy at first. And then it fell apart. Our friends were the collateral damage of our fractured marriage. They chose sides. I suppose they had to. What if we find old friends of theirs and they only remember the bad?"

"It's a chance I'm willing to take. They might remember an imperfect couple who wanted to be together and tried. Besides, they might have been deliriously in love." He didn't know much about Ryder's divorce, but this afternoon's phone call at the skating rink had not boded well.

"What if only one of them tried? But the friends saw things differently?" Ryder handed the photo back to Mason, and he set it on the coffee table. "What if one went into the relationship knowing full well she was not committed to making the marriage work? And the other one found out too late?"

"Our parents didn't get divorced. They died in a car crash."

"You're right." He sighed, raking his fingers through his hair. "I'm just torn up. I don't even recognize my own life anymore."

"I barely recognize mine, either." Mason took a seat on the couch. "So your ex—Lily, right?"

Ryder nodded.

"You must have loved her a lot."

"I did." He slumped in the chair.

"What happened?"

"She fooled me. Used me." He turned his attention to the Christmas tree in the corner.

Mason followed his stare. The white twinkle lights and red and green bulbs were new. He'd left the old ornaments of his and Mia's in the basement. Hadn't had the guts to bring them up.

"When we got engaged, she was wrapping up the final season of *Courtroom Crimes*. She said she was tired of the long hours and needed a break from acting. After the wedding, she wanted children right away. She wanted to be a stay-at-home mom, claimed she had no desire to constantly be on location or work fourteen-hour days. She seemed so loving, so caring. I was ecstatic. I couldn't wait to have kids. A year later, the twins arrived. Within days, she hired a nanny to help out. Again, I understood. Twins, right? But it wasn't until later I found out she was auditioning during the day."

"Was that the deal breaker?" Mason asked.

"No. I admired her talent and always encouraged her to do what she wanted." Ryder hung his head. "I don't know why she kept it all a secret. She got a movie deal when the twins were nine months old. She missed their first birthday. The next year she was barely home, and when she was it was to get ready for this or that event. I didn't love it, but I told myself acting fulfilled her. The twins' third birthday was when everything fell apart. We had a party planned for them, but that morning she announced she'd fallen in love with a producer. A moving company arrived the next day. She moved in with the guy. She couldn't even wait to tell me until after the girls' party."

"Oh, man." Mason rubbed his chin. "I'm sorry. You didn't deserve that."

"Thanks." Ryder closed his eyes and tilted his head back. "I don't know why I can't get over it. I'm so angry, but it doesn't change anything."

"I know anger. But I'm bitter for the opposite reason. I married the perfect girl." He lifted one shoulder in a pointless shrug. "We were happy. In love. Had a baby. She died of cancer. End of story."

"I guess we both loved and lost."

"I reckon you're right."

Neither spoke. Mason's thoughts rearranged themselves again and again. Two weeks ago, he never would have imagined a day like today. He'd gone to Christmas Fest with his brother and nieces. He'd revealed tightly held, cherished memories to his ex-girlfriend. He'd bonded with his twin. And instead of regret or confusion, he'd gained a strong sense of clarity.

His phone dinged. He checked it—Brittany had sent him a text. His pulse took off.

I found some pictures you might be interested in.

He texted her back.

What kind of pictures?

One might be of your parents.

"Ryder, Brittany might have found pictures of our parents."

He leaned forward with excitement. "Tell her to bring them over."

"Now?"

"Yes, now."

After a split second of hesitation, he nodded and texted her.

Are you doing anything now? Want to bring them over?

A few seconds passed. Be there in five.

"She's on her way."

"Here, take these." Brittany handed Mason the albums and took off her coat.

"Hey, Brittany." Ryder grinned behind him. It was funny, but although they were identical, she could easily tell them apart. Their personalities gave them away. Ryder had a more relaxed air to him, and Mason seemed quieter, more intense.

The strange thing? She felt nothing but friendly affection for Ryder. Mason, on the other hand…just looking at him sent a troupe of ballet dancers twirling in her stomach.

They went into the living room and Mason sat on the couch. Brittany sat next to him, and Ryder looked over his shoulder. "What did you find?"

"Nothing. I haven't opened anything yet." Mason rolled his eyes, then met hers. Awareness of him sent tingles over her skin.

"This one can wait." She took the top album and set it on the coffee table. She pointed to the one on his lap. "I found the pictures and clippings in this one."

"Clippings?" He flashed her a questioning glance as he opened it. She refrained from leaning in. She was already too close for comfort as it was. His strong hands, chapped from the cold, mesmerized her.

"How old is this?" Mason got through the first pages quickly.

"I'm not sure. I'm guessing the mid-1980s." She tore her gaze away from his hands. A young guy who looked strikingly similar to Mason and Ryder wore loose-fitting jeans, a short-sleeved shirt, cowboy boots and a cowboy hat. He stood next to a pretty woman with blond hair pulled into a French braid and puffy bangs. She wore a denim miniskirt, a mint-green T-shirt with the sleeves rolled up, matching mint-green socks and white tennis shoes. They stood on Nan's front porch.

"That's our mom." Ryder's voice rose in excitement. "It's the same girl as in your picture."

"What were they doing at Nan's?" Mason's forehead furrowed.

Brittany tried to recall the conversation Mason had had with Nan last week. "Didn't she mention them coming home once?"

"Why wouldn't she have told me they'd stopped by to see her?" His voice rose. "She obviously met them if she took their picture."

"Don't take it personally, Mason. She doesn't remember every little thing."

"It's not a little thing."

"To you, it isn't. But it wouldn't have been a major event for her."

"I don't know." He turned to stare at her. "I can't help thinking maybe you've been right all along, and she's declining quicker than I'd thought."

She bristled. Just because Nan didn't remember something that happened over thirty years ago didn't mean she'd grown senile.

"I was the one who was wrong," she said. "I told you what the doctor said, and the longer I'm here, the more I agree with him."

"Guys?" Ryder made a gesture for him to keep the pages moving.

Mason opened his mouth to say something, then must have thought better of it. He turned the page. And sucked in a breath.

Brittany instinctively placed her hand on his arm. When she'd found the album earlier, she'd almost skipped over the small news clipping. She was glad she hadn't—but she didn't know how either of the men would react to it.

"Is this what I think it is?" Ryder jabbed his finger into the book.

"Yes." Mason lifted it closer to read the small print. "It's a wedding announcement. John Fanning married Lisa Gatlin." He continued to read the small paragraph, then turned to Ryder. "Brian Ditmore and Jennifer Hall were their attendants."

A grin spread across Ryder's face. "We have names."

They high-fived each other, then rose and began to pace in opposite directions. Watching them was bizarre. Their bearing, their gait, even the tilt of their chins was identical. She couldn't look away from them if she tried.

They stopped. Locked gazes.

"I'll hunt down Jennifer's information," Ryder said.

"And I'll track Brian," Mason said.

"We'll get answers," they said simultaneously.

Mason turned to Brittany and held out his hand. She took it and let him help her to her feet. He drew her into a hug. "Thank you."

"You're welcome." She wrapped her arms around him and rubbed his back. All his tender strength made her want to stay in his embrace forever. But he stepped away.

And Ryder took his place. Funny how Ryder's arms

around her should feel the same, but they didn't. She patted his back.

"Want to see the other pictures?" She gestured to the albums. "I didn't find any more of your parents, but there are some classic photos of us as kids."

Ryder scooped up the album from the coffee table and plunked his long frame on the couch.

"This was the summer Mason and I decided we were going to be in the rodeo." She shot Mason a grin, but his expression gave nothing away. "He, of course, was going to be a barrel racer. I, on the other hand, declared I wanted to try my hand at rodeo clown."

"You talked Nan into getting you the makeup." Mason had a soft smile on his face.

"She never could pass up a seventy-five-percent-off sale. I thought I did a good job with the makeup. I begged Nan to take a picture of us."

"The outfit was right," Mason said. "The rest of you was all wrong. And you never had to beg Nan much—she loved taking photos of you."

"True." She laughed. "We brought out a bale of hay from the barn. It was supposed to be our barrel. Then Mason came flying at me on his horse, and instead of running around the hay like I was supposed to, I sprinted to the barn, screaming all the way."

"That was the end of that." Mason chuckled. "I felt bad."

"You did not." She glared at him. "You told me I was a big sissy. I was sure your horse would trample me."

"Well, I was eleven. And too big for my britches. Trying to show off and impress you."

She lowered her chin. "You always impressed me, Mason."

Ryder cleared his throat, gesturing to another picture. "Should I even ask what's going on here?"

Mason leaned in, then guffawed.

"Until tonight, I'd forgotten about this." She and Mason were older in the photo. Probably fourteen.

"Are you wearing a trucker hat, Brittany?" Ryder pressed his lips under to contain his laughter. "And cargo pants?"

"Hey, it was the style." She pretended to be offended. "Just wait until the next page."

"Wait!" Mason held out his hand. "It's not what I'm thinking, is it?"

She gave him her sweetest smile and nodded for Ryder to turn the page.

"Dude!" Ryder let out a chortled laugh.

"Okay, show-and-tell is over." Mason lunged for the album, but Ryder held it up and away from him.

"Are you...a pirate?" Ryder arched his eyebrows, then turned to Brittany. "Is my brother a Jack Sparrow wannabe?"

"I wasn't a pirate. I'm not a wannabe." He tried to grab the album again, but Ryder stood and hugged it tightly.

"To be fair, I only asked him if I could dress him up because I didn't want to go fly-fishing."

"You told me it was an assignment you couldn't get out of." Mason sounded a bit growly.

"For what?" Ryder laughed. "Pirate school?"

"My dance instructor told us to explore the possibilities and to let the world inspire us. Mason and I had gone to see *Pirates of the Caribbean* the night before. And Elizabeth Swann made a huge impression on me. It made me want to choreograph a dance with her as the lead."

"And I, being the nice guy I am, agreed to be Jack Sparrow so she could get into character."

"You were wonderful." She stood and pecked Mason on the cheek.

"Well, you didn't leave me much choice. And I want that picture burned."

Ryder shook his head. "No way. The picture stays."

They sat down and went through the rest of the album. Ryder teased Mason, and Brittany filled in the story gaps. By the time they'd finished, she couldn't suppress her yawns anymore.

"I'm going back." She gathered the albums. "I'll make copies of the wedding announcement and the picture of your parents for you both."

"I'll walk you to the door." Mason followed her to the entrance. She put her coat on and turned to say goodbye.

His expression silenced her, though. His eyes held appreciation. And hunger. For her.

He ran the back of his index finger along the hair next to her face. It sent a shiver down her spine. He moved closer to her. She had to tilt her head to see his face. Whatever she'd been expecting there, she didn't find because he lowered his mouth and her lips parted. He must have taken it as an invitation, and she was thankful he did. Because when his lips touched hers, the past rushed back in a million sensations.

He was better than the pictures, better than the memories.

He was better than she remembered.

She sank into his embrace and kissed him back. His hands tightened around her waist.

How could she have gone all these years without his strength? He'd been her rock growing up. And this—being in his arms, tasting the wild cowboy, the fierce protector, the tender man all in one—made her wonder why she ever thought living in another state would work.

It had been ten long years without those arms around her. She couldn't bear another ten without them.

Could she really go back to California when everything she wanted was right here?

He broke away abruptly and averted his gaze, running his hand through his hair.

"I shouldn't have done that. I shouldn't have..." He was shaking his head with a dazed look on his face.

Her spirits dropped like a stone to the bottom of the ocean. Once again, she was just a big regret to Mason.

"Don't sweat it." She opened the door. "Happens to the best of us."

She slipped out the door and hurried to Nan's truck.

Lord, what's wrong with me? Why do I want the one man I can't have? And why do I think it would be any different this time around if I could? The bank will be calling soon.

As she fired up the truck, she reached the only logical conclusion.

Mason was right. He shouldn't have kissed her.

Chapter Eleven

Mason tried to pay attention to the sermon the next morning in church, but his mind kept bouncing around. Bill had cornered him on the way in, asking him to come out to his ranch this morning to check cattle. He knew what that meant. Bill wanted to speak to him in private. What did his father-in-law need to discuss? Was he going to question his abilities as a father and rancher again? Or had he somehow found out he'd kissed Brittany?

Speaking of Brittany…the woman looked like an adventure waiting to happen two rows up on the other side of the aisle. Sure, she was sitting still as could be, her face glowing as she listened intently. But he knew what lurked beneath her serene expression—possibilities.

After last night's kiss, he could no longer pretend he wasn't affected by her. He also couldn't deny that it was a betrayal of all he held dear. Possibilities and adventures with her were off-limits to him. It would dishonor Mia's memory.

He waited for a pit in his stomach to form, but it didn't.

God, I keep expecting my conscience to kick me around and get me back on track. What am I doing? I shouldn't have kissed Brittany. Was it loneliness? The holidays? It can't happen again. You're the One who got me through the past three years. Please get me through this, too. Just get me through the next week. Brittany will go back in California, and I'll go back to...

An empty house on Friday nights and a pile of bills that would take years to pay off.

"Daddy?" Noah tapped his sleeve. "I'm hungwy."

Mason reached into the small backpack he always brought to church. He handed Noah a baggie of crackers and pulled out two more for Ivy and Harper, who sat on the other side of Noah. Ryder was on the end next to them.

Before the service started, they'd been met by many curious stares. Mason was prepared to be bombarded with questions after. He'd much rather answer questions about his twin than have a private conversation with Bill about who knew what.

Seriously, what did the man want? His tone had been disapproving, but then, it usually was.

The opening strains of "As with Gladness Men of Old" began playing, and he opened his hymnal. As he sang the first verse, he was struck by the message. Christmas was a time for rejoicing, but in the years since Mia had died, he'd stopped rejoicing. Instead, he'd dragged through each day, each season, each holiday.

He'd been barely getting by for a long time.

He longed for something different.

What was he saying? He *had* something different—he had a twin now.

His gaze fell on Brittany. She'd breezed into town and given him his brother. She'd encouraged him to remember Mia. She'd even made it okay to think fondly on all the memories they'd shared as kids.

She'd given him back things that had been lost, and a part of him longed to have her back, too.

No.

He'd had the love of his life—and she'd died.

Besides, Brittany had goals, dreams and plans in California that didn't include him.

He'd get through the holidays. He'd forget about her.

But what if he didn't want to forget about her? She made him feel whole again.

Could he really spend the rest of his life as a hollowed-out shell of the man he used to be?

Whatever happened during the rest of her stay in Rendezvous, Brittany would never forget Mason's kiss from last night. She didn't want to forget it. She wanted to hold it in her hands and tuck it away to the safest place in her heart for proof that once upon a time, she'd mattered to someone.

The poinsettias lining the pulpit and Christmas tree up front made her smile. Christmas was the most wonderful time of the year.

Brittany returned her attention to the pastor's sermon. Something about God's plans being better than our own. He mentioned Mary and Joseph.

At the mention of Jesus's mother, Brittany thought of her own mother and couldn't hold back a grimace. Mom had bailed on her countless times growing up. Her job had always been more important than her daughter, and she'd never let Brittany forget it.

Don't think about Mom. Get out of your head and listen to what the pastor's saying.

"God is mighty and has done great things. Holy is His name," the pastor said. "Let us pray."

She bowed her head. *God, I see the way You've pro-*

tected me all my life. So much of what I want is out of my grasp, though. There's a good chance the bank will call in a day or two and turn me down like all the others did. And I'm almost thirty and I haven't had a lasting relationship with anyone since leaving here ten years ago.

Sometimes she had the feeling if she looked closely at why she wanted a studio, she wouldn't like the answer.

The next hymn started playing, and Nan covered Brittany's hand with hers. "It's good to have you here, honey."

Her heart swelled. She was overlooking one of her biggest blessings. Nan. "I'm very happy to be here. I love you."

When church ended, she helped Nan down the aisle. A swarm of people surrounded Mason and Ryder. Ryder held a twin on each hip, and Mason carried Noah. Their resemblance wasn't as shocking to her now that she'd been around both of them. Brittany hitched her chin to them and smiled.

"Brittany, just the person I wanted to see." Gretchen Sable's face lit up as she approached. "I wanted you to meet my nephew, Judd Wilson."

The man next to Gretchen appeared to be in his early thirties. His chin was ducked in an embarrassed manner. When he met her eyes, he nodded. "Ma'am."

Boy, he was handsome. Pure cowboy with that tangle of dark hair, deep blue eyes, a thin gap between his front teeth and a slight hook to his nose. Too bad she didn't get even a flutter of butterflies.

"Nice to meet you." She pasted on a smile and extended her hand. He shook it.

"Pardon me." He gave her a cursory nod. "I've got pregnant cows to check."

A real romantic. Brittany stifled a chuckle and waved goodbye.

"Judd owns a large cattle ranch south of here, *and* he's single." Gretchen took her by the arm. "Why don't I set you two up on a date?"

"Umm…" She tried not to wince, but was Gretchen serious? The last thing Brittany needed was a blind date here in Rendezvous.

"Let her get through a Sunday service before you start matchmaking, Gretch." Lois unhooked the woman's hand from Brittany's arm. "Sorry about that, darlin'. She worries Judd will never get married if she doesn't intervene soon."

"He's quite handsome," Brittany said. "I'm sure he'll be off the market before you know it."

"He is good-looking. A catch. But I want him to have the right kind of lady." Gretchen's tone reeked of discouragement. "Not like Misty Sandpiper or that Boone girl."

She made a mental note not to ask about the Boone girl, certain it would open an ugly can of worms.

"Which Boone girl?" Nan chimed in.

"The youngest. Stella," Gretchen huffed. "Did you hear what she did last night?"

"What?" Lois was all ears.

"She drove smack into the back end of Dirk Smither's car."

Lois let out a low whistle as she herded them to the coatracks. "She must be getting desperate if she's causing accidents to get his attention."

"Maybe her car hit a patch of ice." Brittany hadn't meant to join the conversation, but there could be an innocent explanation, right?

Lois snorted. "Yeah, like she just happened to lose her dog at Judd's ranch last summer? We all know her Chihuahua is an indoor lapdog. The tiny thing would have been eaten by a coyote before it ever made it six miles to his ranch. And what about her car breaking down right in front of Cash McCoy's house in the fall? What was she doing out on Grizzly Peak Road for her car to break down out there?"

Brittany had to give this Stella credit. The girl sounded inventive. She knew how to get a man's attention.

"I'm glad she's sniffing around Dirk instead of Judd. I wish Gabby would give him a chance, but she's always going on about not dating cowboys. A pity." Gretchen pointed to her. "What this town needs is a nice girl like you, Brittany."

"Wouldn't that be wonderful?" Nan smiled at her.

Gratitude expanded in her chest. They wanted her. How sweet it was to be wanted, even by women her grandmother's age.

Life in Santa Ana didn't seem as satisfying as it used to be. Since Brittany had been here, she hadn't talked to a single person from back home.

No one missed her. And she didn't miss anyone except the girls she taught. But they'd move on as they graduated. They all did.

"You'd have your pick of the cowboys—they need someone smart and pretty and fun like you," Gretchen assured her.

Her pick of the cowboys... Brittany looked backward over her shoulder at Mason. His eyes met hers, and his lips curved in acknowledgment before someone else grabbed his attention.

There was only one cowboy she'd ever wanted.

She still wanted him.

Her heart coiled into a knot.

"I do feel bad for Sandy Boone, though." Lois handed Nan's coat to her. "With Stella acting like a tart and Nicole's husband in the hospital, it's a wonder she's holding it together as well as she is this Christmas."

"Nicole?" Nan asked, buttoning her coat. "The middle girl?"

"Yes. Remember she married the Taylor boy? Aaron?"

Nan looked confused.

"The one who found out he had muscular dystrophy in high school? Nicole and Aaron were inseparable. The whole town knew they'd be together forever by the time they were in third grade."

Gretchen clasped her hands. "I didn't know Aaron was hospitalized. Is it serious?"

"I don't know, but they could sure use our prayers." Lois shook her head. "When I think of Nicole knowing his health problems and marrying him regardless..." She blinked, appearing to be choked up. "That's love."

Whoever this Nicole was, she sounded selfless.

Brittany frowned. She herself was not selfless. She looked out for number one. Had since she was a child.

So why was she trying to choose between warring goals? Studio and dance team or Mason and Nan.

Thrusting her arms into her coat sleeves, she tuned out what the ladies were saying.

She couldn't have it all.

It was like those logic problems she'd never understood in grade school. She could have either this or that. Not this *and* that.

Why was she fooling herself into thinking she could have a future with Mason, anyhow? He was mourning Mia and probably always would be. The first thing he'd done after he'd kissed Brittany last night was regret it.

A brief stint in Rendezvous wasn't going to change a thing.

But...did it have to be a brief stint? This town welcomed her, made her feel different from any place she'd been. And how many years did Nan have left? Did Brittany really want to spend them hundreds of miles away?

She had a lot to think about before Christmas.

"This Ryder character—"

"My brother. My twin brother." Mason gritted his teeth as he toweled off Slick, one of Bill's geldings. They were in Bill's stables, where the familiar smells of hay, horse and earth made him feel at home. He and Bill had checked the cattle briefly, and Bill was finally getting down to the real reason he'd asked Mason over.

"Okay. Your brother. I'm not denying he's your kin." Bill shot him a dark glance. "But what does he want with you? Why now?"

"What do you mean?" Mason already didn't like the direction this conversation was going. He was glad Ryder had stayed home to make a fort in the living room with the kids and do an online search for Jennifer Hall.

"I mean, you own a sizable ranch." Bill grabbed another towel. "Are you certain his coming to town is innocent?"

How was he supposed to respond? The idea seemed ludicrous. "He didn't know I existed until recently. The timing has nothing to do with him wanting my ranch."

"He said he missed ranching." Bill raised his eyebrows.

"So? He grew up on a sheep ranch."

"Look, I know you see the best in people, and that's good. But the blondie from your past shows up with your twin, and now you're all spending time together like you've been best friends since birth. From an outside perspective, it raises concerns."

"Are you suggesting Brittany also wants my ranch?" His tone was clipped, and he didn't care. Bill's derogatory attitude toward Brittany was uncalled-for.

"No, a girl like her would never be happy out here for long. This part of the world is too slow, too lonely for someone like her."

Now his father-in-law was the expert on Brittany? He forced himself to be gentle as he finished up with Slick.

"I don't know why we're talking about it," Mason said. "She's here to visit Nan. She's never once mentioned staying in Rendezvous. And Ryder...well, if he wanted to move here, it would be fine by me."

"You say that now, but what if he laid claim to Fanning Ranch?"

"I guess I'd deal with it if the time came. I mean, he's a Fanning, too. Technically, it should be both of ours."

"But your grandfather left it to you. Only you." Bill shook his head in disgust. "If he wanted Ryder to inherit it, he would have named him in the will. And don't try to feed me some line about him not knowing you had a brother. He must have known."

Irritation spilled into his gut, but he forced himself to keep quiet. What was Bill's problem? They used to have a decent relationship. Mason had relied on him for everything from help with weaning calves to advice about fixing his tractor. Lately, the bond between them had grown brittle. Could it even be restored at this point?

"I'm only bringing this up because it concerns my grandson. Noah deserves to have a profitable ranch when he grows up and takes over. I don't want his success affected by any decisions you make at a vulnerable time."

A vulnerable time? What was that supposed to mean? How much more vulnerable could he have been than right after Mia died? He'd managed to keep the ranch together at that point.

"I appreciate you talking straight with me, Bill, but I've got my affairs under control."

"Look, I'm not blind, Mason. I can see you've been tightening your bootstraps around the ranch. Keeping fewer heifers. Making do with one less ranch hand."

"Yeah, well, that's my business." He thought about the balances on the hospital bills. They no longer kept him up at night because he knew God would take care of him no matter what. He'd worn parts of the Bible thin reading God's promises. No matter how tough things got on the ranch, God would provide a way forward.

"When it involves my grandson, it's my business, too."

"I don't appreciate you implying I'm a deadbeat dad." Mason turned to face him, and he realized it was time. Time to confide in Bill. It wasn't as if the man didn't already think he couldn't handle the ranch. What could it hurt at this point? "After Mia's diagnosis, bills from doctors started pouring in. They didn't stop arriving until a full year after she'd died. I've made arrangements with the hospital and other medical offices, and I'm on a payment plan. But it will be a good long while before they're all paid off."

Bill frowned. "What about your insurance?"

"It covered some." Due to the aggressive nature of Mia's cancer, they'd opted to try expensive experimental treatments. Mason would do it again in a heartbeat. It had given him hope.

"Why didn't you tell me? We would have helped."

"The day I married your daughter, she became my responsibility. I wasn't saddling you and Joanna with my problems when you've got your own future to think about."

"How much are we talking?" Bill seemed subdued.

"I've got it under control." He made his way toward the stable door. "I've got to get back."

"Mason, wait."

He turned.

"I didn't know." Bill seemed to shrink.

"Why would you? I didn't tell anyone. I'll see you later."

As he braced himself against the cold air, he looked to the overcast sky. He frowned, tucking his chin into his coat collar. Telling Bill about the medical bills released something he'd been clinging to, and although he felt lighter, he also felt sad. The glue that had bound him and Mia together seemed to be unraveling.

Right after her death, he'd promised himself he'd never let her go. There would be nobody else for him, because he'd had the best in her.

Mason marched toward his truck.

Where were his promises now?

Weariness crept into his bones. As he drove away, he didn't think, just headed to Nan's. Because now that Bill knew about his finances, Mason wanted to tell Brittany about them, too. He didn't know why. And he didn't care to figure it out, either. He just needed her to know.

Chapter Twelve

"Really? I'll be right over." Brittany ended the call, her insides jiggling with nervous anticipation. After church, she and Nan had joined Lois for a leisurely brunch at Riverview Lounge. Christmas carolers had serenaded each table, and Brittany was truly feeling the Christmas spirit.

Since Nan was sleeping off the biscuits and gravy, Brittany had decided on a whim to call the number listed on the for-sale-by-owner sign of the building in Rendezvous. She figured she'd leave a message, but to her surprise, Babs O'Rourke answered. Turned out, Babs owned the old computer repair shop and wanted Brittany to tour the place right now.

She couldn't pass up the opportunity. Ever since she'd seen the building, the question had been burning.

How much would it cost to have a dance studio here?

Possibilities spun through her mind one after the other as she put on her boots. Every small town had little girls dreaming of tutus and recitals. The problem came when they got older. Sports and band and other activities grabbed their interest. Rendezvous would be the last place she could realistically put together a competitive dance team.

Well, nothing about a dance studio in Rendezvous *realistically* fit in with her goals.

If the bank called and approved her line of credit, she'd lease the building in Santa Ana and have the career she wanted. She'd need to renovate immediately, fully book the classes and gather a dance team in order to afford the rent and pay more dance instructors. Although it might take years for her to make enough profit to get out of her small one-bedroom apartment, it would be worth it. Wouldn't it?

She put on her coat and scribbled a note for Nan before grabbing her purse and heading out the front door. It was a bitterly cold day. Her breath froze in her throat, making her cough. A truck pulled into view.

Mason.

With her hands in her pockets, she shivered on the porch until he parked. As he strode toward her, last night's kiss crashed over and over in her mind.

Why was he so tall? So handsome? So quiet and strong and dependable?

Why, oh why, did she want to throw herself into his arms and kiss him again?

"Hey, do you have a minute?" Mason's eyes swam with vulnerability.

"I'm on my way into town."

"Oh." He stared at his boots.

"You could come with me."

"I'll do that." His throat worked as he swallowed. "Want to take my truck?"

"Sure." Another thing she admired about him—he didn't ask a lot of questions. Just accepted the fact she was going to town and offered to drive.

After buckling her seat belt, she turned to him. "What's going on?"

The tightening of his jaw was his only answer. He started the truck up and steered it back to the main road.

Was he going to lecture her about the kiss? Tell her it was a mistake? That they should avoid each other until she left?

"Before you say last night was a mistake," she said, "I'm going to throw a few things out there. It wasn't some massively big deal. It could have happened to anyone. Hey, there might have been mistletoe hanging up there. I can't be sure." She twisted her hands together.

"Are you done?" The corner of his mouth twitched upward.

"Are you going to lecture me?"

"No. I didn't come here about last night."

"You didn't?" Relief rushed hot and sweet through her veins.

He shook his head, casting a quick peek at her. They reached the main road.

"Where are we going, anyway?" he asked.

"Oh, go to town and take a left on Third Street. I'm meeting Babs O'Rourke at the old computer repair shop."

"Babs? You could have warned me." He took a left. Snowcapped mountains rose to their left, and hilly white pastures rolled to their right.

"You can stay in the truck if you'd like. It won't take long."

"Is this meeting about Nan?"

"No, why?" she asked.

"You told me you'd keep me in the loop."

"I am. I already told you I think she's okay living on her own. For now, at least."

"Good."

"I still want to hire a home health aide to come in once or twice a week to help her shower and to do some light cleaning."

"I'm okay with that."

"And something needs to be done about a power of attorney. If anything were to happen to her or her memory got worse, I wouldn't be able to pay her bills or make decisions about her care."

"If you had power of attorney, would you be able to do all that from California?" The straightforward question wasn't laced with innuendo.

"I don't know. I'd do my best."

"I'll do it," he said. "Gladly."

Just like that. The man was too good to be true.

"But…" He shot her a look full of worry. "You'd have to know something first. It's what I was coming over to tell you. I don't know why it bothers me so much. It's not like I can help it. I don't need advice or anything."

What was on his mind? She'd never seen him so agitated. His thumbs were drumming against the steering wheel faster than her rhythm tap class.

"Just say it."

"I'm in debt."

"Who isn't?" She laughed, but he must not have found it funny.

"The bills will take years to pay off." The planes of his face sharpened. "I don't want the whole town knowing."

Poor Mason. He'd lost his wife. Was deep in debt. He was a proud man—of course he wouldn't want the town knowing. She touched his shoulder. "I understand. I won't tell a soul."

"It's not like I went hog wild or anything. They're medical bills. Left over from…" His throat worked. "Anyhow, cancer treatments aren't cheap, and hospital stays aren't, either. The insurance covered a lot of it, but…"

"You don't have to say anything more, Mason. Last year I broke my toe, and I'm still getting bills. One tiny

X-ray produced five invoices. I got bills from the orthopedic surgeon, the lab where the X-ray was taken, maybe Marie Curie herself for coming up with the technology."

"Yeah, that pretty much sums it up." They reached the outskirts of town. "I cut costs to the bare minimum on the ranch."

"I know you. You honor your debts." She patted his arm. "If it takes years, it takes years. Don't worry. I can only speak from my own experience, but God has stretched my finances again and again."

"He's done the same for me. It gets tight sometimes, but I've managed to keep going."

"I've taken scrimping to a whole new level if you ever need tips." She gave him a teasing grin.

"I might." He smiled briefly. "As far as acting as Nan's power of attorney, I don't want you to think I'd be trying to get anything out of it. I might be in debt, but I would never take advantage of your grandmother."

"The thought would never cross my mind. Never."

They drove down Centennial and took a left on Third Street. Mason parked the truck and shifted to face her.

"I would look out for Nan's best interests. I know you don't want to worry about taking care of her. I just wanted you to know where I stood."

What was that supposed to mean? She would gladly worry about taking care of her grandmother—Nan wasn't a burden. She just wanted to do what was best for her.

Mason still didn't get it—still didn't get her. And it hurt.

"I know where you stand," she said quietly. "I know the foundation you're built on. Each summer I spent every waking minute with you from the time I was four years old until we graduated from high school." She opened the passenger door. "And just so you know, I'm the same girl you grew up with, too. You knew me once upon a time. I'm not trying to push Nan's care onto you. I want to take care of her. Why can't you ever give me the benefit of the doubt?"

She got out of the truck and slammed the door behind her.

"Brittany, wait." Mason jogged to the sidewalk where she'd stormed off. He caught her by the arm. "That came out wrong."

She shook his hand away.

"Howdy, you two!" Babs waved as she strolled toward them. Her red ski jacket was only slightly brighter than her hair. She winked at Brittany. "I didn't know you were bringing your beau."

"He's *not* my beau." Brittany flicked him a cool look. "What can you tell me about this place?"

He wanted to growl, but instead, he had to stand there and not let his emotions take over.

"Whatever you say, hon." Grinning, she jangled a set of keys and strode to the door. "Ted Wilder bought it almost ten years ago when everyone and their brother was getting a virus on their computer. But with laptops coming down in price so much, a lot of folks stopped getting them repaired and just bought new ones…so he shut 'er down. After my Herb died, I went on a real estate tear— snatched the place up along with three other empty buildings around town. But you know, I'm getting old, honey. I don't want the hassle of owning all this stuff anymore."

Mason wasn't sure what to do. Follow them into the building or wait in his truck? Brittany was mad at him, but it wasn't his fault. She'd misread his words.

When Babs unlocked the glass door, he held it open for them.

Decision made. He was going in.

"This building was an insurance agency for years before Ted took over," Babs said. "It's also been a record store and a vacuum repair shop. Been sitting empty going on two years. I was going to open one of those make-it-and-paint-it pottery shops, but I didn't have the heart. Starting businesses with Herb was fun, but without him? It's not the same."

Mason hung back. Why was he here? He should be back home with Ryder and the kids. He'd said what he'd wanted to say to Brittany. And more.

He sighed. He'd hurt her feelings.

"Are there any dance studios in town?" Brittany glided to the front counter, then rose on her toes and pivoted on one foot to take in the space. Her graceful movements brought a funny sensation to the back of his neck.

Wait. Why was she asking about dance studios? A burst of hope filled his heart, but he beat it down as best he could.

"I thought you were buying a place in California." He tried to keep his tone nonchalant.

She blushed. Babs wisely excused herself, but Mason knew the woman was hanging on their every word. He crossed over to stand near Brittany.

"I wanted to see how the prices compared." She wouldn't look at him as she shrugged.

"And how do they compare?" he asked quietly. A storm was brewing inside him, and he wasn't sure if it was due to the way she hadn't judged him for his debts, her fiery speech about knowing him, the fact she'd called him out a few minutes ago or…

Was she considering moving to Rendezvous?

For good?

The thought was so appealing, he thought his legs might give out.

"I don't know. Babs and I haven't gotten around to prices." She pushed against his chest and stepped past him to signal to Babs. He didn't try to stop her. Why would he? If she liked the price, she might stay, and if she stayed, he'd get to see her whenever he wanted.

Every day.

He'd have his friend back.

Yeah, like you really think of her as a friend.

"Honey, I won't lie to you, it doesn't have much in the way of character—but it's a good space. You can see how large it is." Babs gestured for her to follow. "Come on, I'll show you the office and bathroom. Oh, and no, we don't have any dance studios in town. Nearest one is over an hour away."

He didn't consider himself the nosy type, but he followed them to the back. No way was he missing a word.

"Are you willing to lease out the building?" Brittany craned her neck to check out a counter.

"No, honey, I'm not. I've already sold the other properties. This is my last one, and once it's gone, my landlady days will be over."

"Everything is really outdated." Brittany tapped her chin.

"A couple coats of paint and it will be fresh as a daisy." Babs pulled a sheet out from the folder she carried and handed it to Brittany. "Did I mention there's a one-bedroom apartment upstairs? You could live in it or rent it out. It's up to you. My nephew lived there for a while, but he moved to Montana this summer."

"An apartment?" Brittany brightened. "Can I see it?"

"Of course, honey. Let me find the key."

Mason sidled next to Brittany and scanned the sheet.

"Babs?" Brittany's voice had a mangled quality. "Is this the price?"

The lady craned her neck to see where Brittany was pointing.

"Yes, hon, the price is negotiable. Don't let it scare you off."

"This isn't missing a zero at the end?" Brittany seemed fixated on the paper.

"Missing a zero?" Babs barked out a laugh. "Around here? Unless this place has grazing land I don't know about, the price is correct. Now let me show you the rest…"

They made their way to the office, poked through the closets and bathroom, then went out the back door and up a flight of stairs. Babs unlocked the apartment, chattering all the way. "You know, if you made the store into a dance studio, you could offer exercise classes. Jeanette Denroy started a Jazzercise class a few years ago, but since she had the baby, she stopped teaching. That class was packed. She's a nice gal. Never made us feel bad about ourselves for not keeping up. If you could have seen me, you'd have busted a gut, honey. And I know what you're thinking—no, I did not wear a leotard."

Brittany glanced at him with twinkling eyes. Her cheeks were flushed, and her steps light. She looked like she was gliding on air. He wanted to take her in his arms and glide with her.

"Oh, wow, this is a great space," she said. "I didn't think it would be this big."

He curled his lips under at the old, stained carpet and dingy walls. The bones of the place seemed fine. The small galley kitchen was outdated, but there were windows in every room, and Brittany was right, the place was big. While she asked Babs about the parking situation and utilities, he went downstairs to check the electrical system and pipes. Everything seemed to be in order.

A few minutes later, Brittany and Babs came back down.

"I've got the papers here if you're ready to make an offer." Babs tapped the folder.

"I'll have to think about it. Thank you so much." Brittany hugged the woman. "I really appreciate you taking time out of your Sunday to show this to me. I'm sure you have a million things to do this close to Christmas."

"I'm happy to do it, and I've been ready for Christmas for three weeks. You let me know if you have any questions or want to stop by again."

"I will."

Mason trailed behind them as they exited. Babs locked it back up and waved goodbye.

He opened the passenger door for Brittany and shut it after she'd climbed up. Then he jogged around and got in. "I didn't realize you were looking at buildings around here."

"I didn't, either." A small smile played on her lips as she kept her attention on the front window.

"Have you heard from the bank in California?"

"No."

"Then…why?"

"Don't worry, Mason." She faced him then, her eyes wavering between hope and pain. "I'm just dreaming. The chances of me moving here are slim to none."

Slim to none. Bill was right. Brittany belonged somewhere else—somewhere busy and warm, with lots to do. He backed out of the spot, thinking of what she'd told him last week at Nan's. How she couldn't have stayed here when she was eighteen.

He'd always known it, but he'd never admitted it.

"I don't blame you for not wanting to move here when you're living the dream in California."

"Living the dream…" she said under her breath. "Not

even close. Sometimes I'm not even sure…" She clamped her mouth shut.

What wasn't she sure of?

"What were you going to say?" He drove down Third Street.

"I don't know if it's worth it when my dreams always go bust. My dream was to be a professional dancer, and I gave it up. I thought putting together a dance team— teaching the best of the best—would be my new dream. But I don't know anymore. Nan's old, and I'm not getting any younger, either."

Were those tears glistening under her lashes? His gut curdled. Maybe she'd been right before—maybe he hadn't given her the benefit of the doubt. It had been easier to believe she was happy, fulfilled, than to think otherwise.

What had it cost her to leave Rendezvous ten years ago? At the time, he'd thought nothing. But now? He studied her profile, and he saw the things she wasn't saying. How much Nan meant to her, how disappointed she was to not be further ahead with her professional plans, and how hard she'd worked to get where she was.

There was more there, too. And he recognized it instantly.

Loneliness.

Never in a million years would he have believed Brittany Green could be lonely. The woman exuded joy—people were drawn to her. She *couldn't* be lonely.

Deep down, though, he knew she was. She'd said she knew him, and he guessed he knew her, too. A decade couldn't erase their connection.

Suddenly, her moving to Rendezvous didn't seem so outlandish.

"Maybe I should be thankful." Her voice sounded scratchy.

"Hey, I'm sorry. I didn't realize…" He didn't know what to say. She seemed to see herself through a different lens than he did. And he didn't like it. "Look, you were right earlier. I haven't given you the benefit of the doubt. You should be proud of what you've accomplished. I know it hasn't been easy for you. You've sacrificed a lot."

"What have I accomplished?" she said under her breath, shaking her head.

"You've taught a lot of kids how to dance. I know how much joy it brings to you. You've passed it on to them. You don't have to teach the best of the best to be important."

She didn't answer, but her frown deepened.

"What more do you want?" He held his breath, hoping he'd hear what he'd wanted to hear ten years ago. The same thing, as much as he tried to deny it, that he wanted to hear now.

His name.

"Everything," she whispered.

The letdown was swift and hard.

They were right back where they'd been. If she got the line of credit—if she had to make a choice between her career and him—she'd choose the studio and the dance team in California.

Nothing had changed.

He should be glad. Should be thankful he wouldn't have to break his promise. There would be no other woman for him besides Mia.

But the emptiness inside him grew bigger.

Mia's memory was all he had to keep him warm.

And right now he was colder than he'd ever been.

Chapter Thirteen

"Being here with you has got me thinking." Brittany was surrounded by wrapping paper, ribbons, bows and tape on Nan's living room floor on Monday. A radio station played Christmas music in the background, and the room smelled of cinnamon from the rolls they'd baked earlier. Snow fell in big flakes outside the windows. Everything about this moment wrapped her up in the Christmas feels.

"What's that, dear?" Nan handed her a sheet of name tags.

She hesitated. Maybe it wasn't the right time. Maybe she should wait to discuss the future with Nan until *after* she was certain about what she wanted to do.

Last night she'd barely slept. She'd done a quick analysis of dance centers in similarly sized small towns across Wyoming and figured out her income requirements for opening a studio here. The numbers had been surprising—shocking, even. She'd only need a small loan to purchase the computer repair shop and make renovations. She could either live in the apartment or rent it out. She could have a comfortable life here. But it would mean giving up the idea of the competitive dance team.

Stripping away the dance team meant giving up on another big goal.

She'd be just another dance teacher in just another town.

Ripping off a piece of tape, she smoothed it on the wrapping paper of the box of candy Nan had bought for Mason. His words from yesterday kept running through her brain. *You don't have to teach the best of the best to be important.*

It sounded right, so why did she think he was wrong? What was she trying to prove to herself? She had to stop thinking about it.

"I've enjoyed spending this time with you."

"Me, too." Nan brightened. "I always love it when we're together. How I would look forward to our summers together! I would cry when you left."

"Really?" Her heart squeezed. "I looked forward to our summers together, too. You made me feel special—loved."

"You are special." Nan gave her a tender smile. "And loved."

"I feel the same about you. I'm sorry I haven't been around much." Brittany shifted to sit cross-legged. "I know Mason comes over every day, but I've been thinking it might be smart to have someone else come in a few times each week, too."

"I don't want strangers here." She shook her head.

No shock there. Brittany reached for the toy tractor she'd bought for Noah. "It wouldn't be a stranger. You know Vera Wick."

"Vera?" Her expression loosened. "From church?"

"Yes. She could use a little extra money, and she does light cleaning for a few other ladies in town." Brittany kept her tone as light as a feather. "She'll even help them shower if they're nervous about slipping."

"I don't need help showering."

"I know. I'm just telling you what I heard." Brittany unrolled paper with puppies in red bows and cut a portion off. "Anyhow, money's tight for her, and it would make me feel better knowing we could help out Vera, and then you wouldn't have to clean the house."

"I suppose it wouldn't hurt if she needs the money..." Nan picked up the fluffy stuffed kitten Brittany had bought for Ivy and set it on her lap.

Relief ran down her spine, but she schooled her face to conceal her emotions. If she went back to Santa Ana, at least she'd have some assurance Nan wouldn't be alone so much. But that was assuming she left...

Could she broach the subject she wasn't sure about at all? She stretched her arm to one side then the other. Took her time wrapping Noah's gift before reaching for the butterfly net she'd bought Harper.

Come on, Brit. Think about what Lois said. You owe it to Nan to find out what she wants before making any decisions.

"You wouldn't believe where my head went this week." Her voice sounded high even to her own ears. "I saw a building for sale downtown, and on a whim, called the number. And what do you know, Babs O'Rourke owns it. That's where I went while you were napping yesterday. It used to be the computer repair center. It needs renovations, but something about it spoke to me. Do you know the place?"

"I'm not sure." Nan wrapped the stuffed animal in tissue paper.

"I guess it was a vacuum shop, then an insurance agency."

"The vacuum shop? Oh, yes, it was the record store. On Third Street. Your grandfather and I used to go there and buy albums. I couldn't wait to get the new Frank Sinatra records, but Neil liked the country artists. By the time Joanie was in high school, the shop had been sold. A shame. I think she would have liked it."

"What was she like in high school?" Why had her mother hated Rendezvous so much?

Nan's face fell. "I should have put more limits on her. Neil and I, well, we tried for so long to have children. I'm afraid we spoiled her." She carefully placed the stuffed animal into a gift bag. "She was full of imagination as a child, and she had high expectations."

Her mother did have high expectations. Brittany wouldn't argue with that.

"She was going to be an astronaut. Then it was a movie star. Then a lawyer to fight for the down-and-out."

Fighting for the down-and-out? Didn't sound like her mother at all. She'd devoted her career to being a corporate consultant to boost profits, which meant cutting costs—and sometimes jobs.

"I encouraged her to dream big. Figured it couldn't hurt anything," Nan continued. "But she changed in high school. She got a chip on her shoulder. Had nothing but bad things to say about this town. Neil and I chalked it up to teenage foolishness. Then she fell in love. She was eighteen. She'd already been admitted to UCLA."

Had this been the guy who shattered her mom's dreams? Brittany knew her father hadn't—Mom had been clear on that point.

"With who?" Brittany asked. "What happened?"

"Wes was a cowboy who worked on a local ranch during the summer. He moved here to be closer to the rodeos.

He was a bull rider. She went to all of the events and watched him compete. He was a gem."

"So he broke her heart?" Sympathy for Mom hit unexpectedly.

"Joanie?" Nan chuckled. "He wanted her to move down to Texas and ranch with him. She wanted him to come to Los Angeles with her."

"The cowboy said no, huh."

"Oh, no. He was smitten. He followed her to LA."

"He did?" It didn't add up to any concrete picture of her mother she'd put together. "Then why did she always tell me her dreams died here?"

"She told you that? I don't know. It seems to me her dreams were alive and well here. If she hadn't gotten it in her head she had to have an important job to be happy, I think she would have married Wes and been fulfilled."

Have an important job to be happy? The phrase sank to her gut.

Nan made a tsk-tsk sound. "That poor young man. He didn't have a chance. A cowboy in Los Angeles? If she thought Rendezvous was backward, you can imagine how she viewed Wes when he came to town. I think she broke his heart, and she broke her own in the process."

Her mother had lied to her! All the lectures about Rendezvous being a dream killer…why had her mom done that? Why hadn't she told her the truth?

"I can't believe it." Brittany shook her head. "Mom was always warning me about this town and living out in the middle of nowhere."

"Doesn't surprise me. The older you got, the less she wanted you to come here for the summers."

"Really? I didn't know that."

"She and I had awful rows. When she broke up with

Wes, I told her I thought she was making a big mistake. He was her true love. And she told me to mind my own business. I probably should have. Our relationship never fully healed, but at least she didn't keep you from me. Maybe if I would have given her more responsibilities growing up, she would have gotten a sense of identity without having to find it in her career."

The butterfly net fell out of Brittany's hand to the floor.

I'm just like my mother.

She scrambled to her feet and crossed over to the window. Shifting back and forth from foot to foot, she tried to find her equilibrium.

She'd been trying to find her identity in her career for ten years. How many times had she told herself she'd have time for a serious relationship *after* she owned a studio and put together a dance team? How many dates had she turned down to work an extra shift for the down payment? How many vacations had she brushed off?

Her breathing came in shallow gasps, and she kept her gaze trained on the snowy prairie outside.

What would it take for her to feel like she'd made it?

And would anyone be there to celebrate with her when she did?

I have to change. I want more—so much more—than Santa Ana can give me.

She whirled to face Nan. "How would you feel if I moved here?"

"What do you mean?"

"I'm seriously considering buying that store and turning it into a dance studio."

"I don't understand." Nan had a look of wonder on her face. "Would you really move here?"

"I might. I don't know yet." She went over to the couch and sat next to her. "If I did, how would you feel about it?"

"It would be a dream come true. You could stay with me." Nan patted her cheek. "You can have your old room."

"You wouldn't mind?"

"Mind? It would make me so happy!"

"The building has an apartment. I could live there."

"If you need your space…"

"I don't. I just wouldn't want to impose on you."

"You could never impose on me." Nan held both hands in hers. Her smile made her look young again. "Have you told Mason? He'll be so pleased."

"I haven't." She pulled her hands away.

"Why don't you go over there and tell him? He's been waiting for you."

"No, he hasn't. He's still grieving his wife."

Nan waved dismissively. "He hasn't had a reason to stop. It would do him a world of good to have you around."

Brittany's cell phone rang. "Excuse me a minute." She answered it and moved to the kitchen.

"Miss Green?"

"Yes, this is she."

"Jerry Moore here. I'm pleased to tell you your line of credit has been approved…"

She'd gotten the line of credit? Mr. Moore gave her the details. She went through the motions, asked the right questions and quickly ended the call in a daze.

This meant she could open the studio in Santa Ana—it was everything she'd worked for, everything she'd wanted for years.

Except now she didn't want it at all.

She laughed. She wanted to move here. Be part of a

community. Be close to the people who mattered to her the most.

Before she could talk herself out of it, she texted Mason.

Are you busy? Can I come over?

He responded instantly.

Come over. The kids want to show you their fort.

She had one more call to make first. She dialed Babs O'Rourke.

She was moving to Rendezvous no matter what Mason had to say.

Mason stood back as Brittany squeezed between the twins and Noah in the fort they'd made. Noah had grabbed her hand the instant she arrived and dragged her to the living room. Mason had made the smart choice to stay outside the fort. Being within two feet of her put his senses on high alert.

"I love it! It's so spacious." Brittany made it sound like she was visiting Buckingham Palace. "I could take a nap in here."

"We should make popcorn!" Noah yelled.

"It's only two sleeps till Christmas!" Harper shouted.

"I hope Santa brings me a kitty," Ivy said, her tiny voice tinkling. "It could sleep with me, and I'd pet it and hold it and—"

"Santa said no pets this year." Ryder lifted the edge of one of the blankets. "Brittany, did Mason tell you we found Jennifer Hall?"

"No, he didn't." Brittany crawled out through the flaps of the overlapping blankets. As soon as she emerged, she straightened and pressed her hands behind her back to work the kinks out. "Have you talked to her?"

"She's calling tonight," Ryder said.

"I'm glad. You'll finally get some answers."

"We hope so," Mason said. "Is something going on?"

She flashed her ocean blues his way. Something was on her mind, and he had a bad feeling about it.

"Remember how I used to help you muck stalls on Saturday mornings so we'd have the whole day together?" Something told him she wasn't tripping down memory lane just for fun. She stretched her neck from side to side. "Can we go out there? I'd like to see the stables again."

"I guess." He glanced at Ryder, who raised his eyebrows like he had no clue, either. "Do you mind watching the rug rats for a little bit?"

"Not at all."

He and Brittany put on their coats and boots and tromped outside. A steady snow was falling. The stables were just up ahead. He opened the door and waited for her to enter before him. A whinny and the low stomp of a hoof told him everything was fine in here.

"Is Nan okay?"

"Oh yeah, she's fine. I almost talked her into coming, but she wanted to stay inside where it was warm." She paced ahead, then turned to him. "So anyway, it's been um…different being back here, and yesterday made me consider things I never imagined. This morning Nan and I made cinnamon buns, and it was really fun and I thought how nice it would be to do it more often. She's getting so old, and who knows how long she'll live?" She paused and, shivering, wrapped her arms around herself.

He had no idea where she was going with this, but at the sight of her shivering, he wanted to warm her up.

"I had an inspiration. I was getting ready to wrap

Harper's present—I hope she loves it because the girl has a lot of energy—and Nan started talking about when my mother was a teen. Mom always pounded it into my head how bad this town was and how dreams can't come true here, but according to Nan, Mom never even tried to make her dreams come true here. She sprinted away as soon as she graduated from high school and never looked back. Then Nan said something else and…well, I won't go into details, but I felt beaten with a truth stick."

Beaten with a truth stick?

"I can't believe I'm saying this, but I'm moving to Rendezvous."

Moving to Rendezvous?

He took two steps backward and almost tripped over a bucket. Panic laced with adrenaline, and he opened his mouth to speak but had no idea what to say.

"I'm buying the computer repair store. I'm remodeling it to be a dance studio. I know I won't be able to have a competitive dance team here, but I'll be able to teach kids. You're right. Teaching kids how to dance brings me joy. Plus, I'm a licensed fitness instructor, so I can offer adult classes, too."

"Why?" It was the only word his mouth would form.

"Because this town feels like home. I want to be near Nan." She dropped her chin, then met his eyes with an intensity he couldn't ignore. "I want to be near you."

It was all happening too fast. He tore off his gloves and ran his fingers over his hair. "But the line of credit… the studio in California…"

"I don't want it."

"When it gets approved, you'll change your mind."

"It already was approved. I got the call before I came over."

His head spun with too many emotions. Hope. Fear.

Denial. And he closed his eyes for a moment, remembering her wistfulness as she'd talked about putting together a dance team. That was what she really wanted.

"Don't do it." He didn't mean to sound harsh.

"What?" Her face blanched. "Why not?"

"Because you'd be giving up what you really want."

"If I stay in California, I'd be giving up something else I want." Her sincerity clouded his thinking.

He wasn't ready. Couldn't think.

A relationship with Brittany could not happen. No way. *Why can't it?*

"I told you, I'll take care of Nan. You don't have to worry." He knew deliberately misreading her words would hurt her, but it had to be done.

"I wouldn't just be giving up Nan, Mason." She moved forward until she stood directly in front of him. Her face tipped up. Two inches, maybe one, separated them. His heart pounded. "I love you."

Love. It ripped the breath from his lungs.

"No." He shook his head, looking anywhere except at her. "We cared about each other a long time ago, but we both got over it. I married Mia…"

But he could finally admit he was lying to himself.

He did love Brittany.

He'd always loved her.

I've got to do the right thing. Mia deserves better than this.

"I know you loved Mia," she said gently. "She'll always have a special place in your heart. I would never expect it to be otherwise. Look, I know you're not ready for this conversation. I'm not trying to freak you out. I just wanted you to know I'm moving back."

"I don't think you should. I… I won't ever be ready for this conversation, because Mia was it for me, okay? She was the love of my life. End of story." Emotion pressed hard and hot against the backs of his eyes, but he suppressed it. His lips were saying the right words, but his heart didn't feel them. Not anymore. "When you get back to California, you'll snap out of wanting to live here. You'll remember why you wanted the dance team and how hard you've worked to open the studio. These feelings? They're nothing."

"They're not nothing." She looked ready to shatter. "Okay. I got the message. Merry Christmas, Mason."

And he let her walk out of the stables. Every step she took away from him felt like a knife to the chest.

He welcomed the pain. It would be best for them both if she walked out of his life for good.

Numbness overtook her as she drove away. At least she knew how Mason really felt.

Mia was the love of his life. He didn't have room for anyone else.

Why had he assumed she'd made the decision to move here lightly? Did he think she'd honestly give up her dream on a whim? Sure, she'd only been here a short while, and the idea had come to her practically overnight. But it didn't mean she was rushing it.

All the disappointments, struggles and closed doors of the past decade had led her to this decision.

Her throat was thick, mangled with tension. Maybe it was for the best. She was used to being alone. Had spent the past decade by herself. She'd renovate the computer repair store, advertise her new studio, spend time with Nan...

Did Rendezvous still make sense if Mason didn't want her here?

A big part of the lure was Mason. Hanging out with him. Dating him.

Having a future with him and Noah.

She pressed on the accelerator. No more useless fantasy thinking.

Rendezvous had more to offer than Mason. It had Nan. And a building she could afford. Mason would have to deal with the fact she was moving back. He didn't have to like it.

The snow-covered landscape rolled by, lonely and bare like her heart.

He was wrong about her changing her mind. She belonged in Wyoming. She could feel it in her bones, in her muscles, in her soul. She felt so strongly about relocating here, she'd choreograph a routine on the spot if a floor was available.

She was done with California. And it wasn't only due to missing Nan or her feelings for Mason. She wanted to get absorbed into a community. She wanted to help Lois and Gretchen and Nan at bake sales and have Sunday brunch at Riverview Lounge.

She'd get over Mason. She had mistaken their friendship for more. She'd read his signals wrong. Attraction plus loneliness did not equal love.

He'd loved Mia. No one questioned it. Certainly not her.

But she couldn't compete with his dead wife.

And he wouldn't let her if she could.

Oh, Mason, if you'd give us a chance, you'd realize I'd never expect you to forget her. I wouldn't ask that of you.

The pressure in her lungs was unbearable. She was practically choking on her battered heart.

Taking deep breaths, she tried not to cry.

She'd finally put her career in its proper place. And she'd still lost the only man who held her heart.

Rendezvous really was a middle-of-nowhere town where dreams died.

Well, so what?

Her dreams hadn't come true anywhere else, either. She might as well accept the fact she would never have Mason. His heart had been buried with Mia long ago.

Chapter Fourteen

As the sun came up the next morning, Mason picked his way through the cemetery. Christmas Eve promised to be clear. No clouds in sight. The only storm whipping was the one in his heart.

Between Brittany's declarations and what he and Ryder had learned from Jennifer Hall last night, he hadn't slept a wink. When Jennifer called, Ryder had put the phone on speaker. What she'd told them was sad but not surprising.

Lisa had confided to her that both of their parents had disapproved of their marriage. Apparently, Ma and Pops had looked down on Lisa because her parents were sheep ranchers. They accused her of stealing their son away from his rightful place on the ranch. And John had felt even less welcomed in her family after being called the son of thieves on account of being a cattle rancher. Lisa and John had hoped things would be less strained as time wore on, but they hadn't even invited their parents to the wedding, knowing it would cause too much drama.

After the private memorial service, Jennifer tried to contact their grandparents a few times, but no one replied to her letters or calls. She'd gotten choked up on the phone when she realized Mason and Ryder had been separated.

Her only guess was the grandparents must have decided it would be better for everyone if they each took a twin and went their separate ways.

The theory made sense, but it didn't make it any easier to swallow. Mason didn't even care what their reasoning was at this point. It didn't change the fact he'd never get those lost years with Ryder back.

Just like he wouldn't get the lost years with Brittany back.

She hijacked his every thought.

The need to confess to Mia choked him, gripped him. He quickened his pace. Her gravestone was up ahead. Someone was stooped over it. Bill?

Mason stopped. Should he leave his father-in-law in peace? Retrace his steps and come back later? Or acknowledge his presence?

Bill looked up then and rose, straightening. Mason forged forward and was shocked when Bill pulled him into a hug, then wiped under his eyes with a handkerchief.

"I owe you an apology, son." He kept one hand on Mason's shoulder. His eyes glistened with tears. "The Lord's been convicting me."

He didn't know what to say. He'd never seen his father-in-law like this.

"I've been holding on too tight." Bill nodded, sniffing. "The last thing I meant to do was push you away, but that's what I've done. Don't say anything. We both know I'm right." He glanced at Mia's headstone. "She was my firstborn. Sweetest thing I'd ever seen. Those pigtails would come flying toward me every time I'd come inside after a hard day of ranching. I'd toss her in the air and her giggles filled my heart. I was glad when you married her. Real glad. I don't think I ever told you that."

Stunned, Mason stood there. He'd always struggled to live up to Bill's expectations.

"I knew you were a hard worker, trustworthy and, best of all, local. You weren't taking my daughter away to another county or worse, another state. You were keeping her on a ranch right here in Rendezvous. No man could have been so blessed as I was. I know you loved her. And I know she loved you."

"I did." His voice scratched. "I do."

"And then we got a grandson, and I tell you it was the best gift I ever could have been given. I love that boy. But after Mia passed…" He dropped his head. "I didn't know it, but I was scared. Scared of losing him, too."

Mason put his hand on Bill's shoulder. "He's fine. Healthy as can be."

"Not like that." He looked away. "You'll find someone else. We won't be part of his life like we've been."

"You will." He tightened his jaw. "You don't have to worry about that."

"I'm not going to worry about it anymore, because it isn't fair to you." He sighed. "I can't stop change, and I'm tired of trying. I've got to move on from losing her. I've got to heal. And I need to let you heal, too."

The quickening of his heartbeat confused him. What was Bill getting at?

"Mia's gone, Mason. You'll see her in heaven. We all will. But until then, we need to make the most of this life we've been given. I talked to Joanna. We're making some changes—nothing set in stone, mind you—but we can't live in the shadow of her death any longer."

He couldn't catch his breath. What was Bill saying? Why now?

"We had money set aside for Mia to go to college, but she chose not to. Joanna and I want you to have it—to pay her medical bills. I don't know what kind of total you're looking at but I hope it covers the balance. If there's any left over, use it for your ranch."

"I can't—"

"You can." Bill clapped him on the shoulder. His eyes were bright with love. "You'll always be the son I never had. Take the money, and let Mia go. She'd want you to be happy. And we do, too." He shifted to leave.

"Bill, wait." His mind swam with questions, but he'd figure out the answers later. Right now he had to say what was on his mind. "You've been like a father to me. I will never take Noah away from you. You're his family—you're my family. No matter what happens, we have each other. You'll always be his grandfather."

A fat tear dropped onto Bill's cheek as his face broke into a grin. He lifted his hand in a half wave, half salute. "I love you, Mason."

"I love you, too."

"We'll see you tonight at the Christmas Eve service." And Bill walked away.

As soon as he was out of sight, Mason collapsed onto his knees in front of Mia's grave. His mind clattered with conflicting thoughts and emotions. His chest ached. And the echoes of Bill's words ripped open the truth he'd been avoiding for too long.

"I'm sorry, Mia." He covered his face with his gloved hands. "I didn't mean to let you down. I retrace those years and think I could have done something to save you. What did I miss? Why couldn't we have found out you had cancer before you were pregnant? But, Mia, our son is beautiful. He's got your cheekbones. He's full of spirit and energy. You'd be so proud of him."

Tears streamed from his eyes and he didn't care.

"We've all had a hard time without you. It about killed

me the first year. And now it's so hard—and I don't even want to tell you this—but I can't remember what your voice sounds like anymore. I strain to hear your laugh… I can't. And it scares me."

He tried to breathe. "The worst thing—and I know it's unforgivable, I know it is—I've fallen in love with Brittany Green all over again. No, I didn't talk to you about her. I'm well aware I made her off-limits as a topic of conversation when you and I were together. I guess that alone should have warned me. I never really got over her."

His heart was being wrung out and guilt overwhelmed him. *God, help me tell her the rest.*

"I can't keep my promise. I'm in love with Brittany, Mia. I'm not the man I thought I was."

His shoulders shook as he sobbed. Snow seeped through the knees of his jeans, and the frigid air sent tremors through his body.

"Forgive me." He stood and raised his head to the sky. "God, forgive me."

He hadn't felt this drained in a long time.

"Forgive me," he whispered, dropping his chin. "Merry Christmas, Mia." He closed his eyes and tried to picture her. Her smiling face was vivid. "You're a hard person to let go."

As he strode back to his truck, the oppressiveness of the past years lifted, and he knew he was going to be all right.

Brittany held a mug between her hands as she watched the sunrise outside the living room window. Sitting cross-legged on a chair, wrapped in a blanket with an unopened Bible in her lap, she let her thoughts scatter. Didn't even try to hold on to them as they darted here and there.

A terrible sense of loss permeated her, but at the same time, hope and clarity kept her from falling apart.

It didn't seem possible today was Christmas Eve. Her life, her entire reason for being, had shifted since arriving here. There wasn't a doubt in her mind that moving was the right decision. Too bad she had doubts about everything else.

She turned her attention to the Bible. Her Bible. A gift to herself five years ago when she'd joined a large church in Santa Ana. Before then, she'd been distant with God, figuring life out for herself. The first time her loan application had been rejected, she'd fallen to her knees and prayed. The prayers led to buying the Bible, and the Bible led to going to church. All had given her the strength to keep saving, to keep her dream alive.

Did I get it all wrong, Lord? Why did I put my life on hold all those years if I was going to end up here, anyhow?

She thought of Charles and the handful of guys she'd barely dated. Had she really put her career first? Or had it been an excuse to avoid having a relationship?

I didn't give them a chance. I used the excuses of saving for the studio and my side jobs to hold them at bay.

Why? Why had she done that?

The answer was there, somewhere. She opened the Bible. Might as well read the Christmas story instead of wallowing in whys. As she turned the pages, her gaze fell on the passage the pastor had discussed on Sunday. *For He that is mighty hath done to me great things; and holy is His name.*

Closing her eyes, she went back—all the way back—to the night she and Mason had broken up so spectacularly. For years she'd berated herself for causing him pain.

She'd held back from love. Convinced herself dance was the only avenue for happiness.

And God had worked it all out, anyway. She didn't begrudge Mason marrying Mia. If not, he wouldn't have Noah. And she didn't regret her own path, either.

If she hadn't struggled these past ten years, she wouldn't have gotten back into praying, or reading the Bible or relying on God. She also wouldn't have worked as hard as she had—soon she'd be the proud owner of a dance studio.

God *had* done mighty things for her.

Maybe she was ready for it now—ready for Rendezvous in a way she hadn't been ten years ago. One thing she knew for sure? She would never find her identity in leading an elite dance team or even owning a studio. And she wouldn't find it in Mason, either.

Lord, strip it all away, and I'm still Yours. I don't need a studio or a dance team or even a husband. All I really need is You.

The beauty of His grace brought tears of gratitude, of regret, of love. She was going to be okay.

As Mason drove away from the cemetery, he prayed out loud.

"God, sometimes I feel like You don't let me have the things I want most." As soon as the words were out of his mouth, he let out a deep breath. *Here we go.*

"It seems like I'm always waiting for the next catastrophe. I know I need to have faith, but I can't stop this fear inside me."

No one else was on the road. He noted the cattle in the distance as he tried to get his thoughts together.

"I'm afraid, God. I'm afraid of letting Brittany in and losing her, too. I'm afraid of falling so hard I won't be able to pick myself up if You take her to be with You the way You did with Mia."

He'd survived ten years without Brittany. He'd married, had a child and buried his wife.

"And I'm more confused than ever because what Bill said back there—it shocked me. Is he right? Would Mia want me to be happy—with another woman? I can't imagine it."

What if he had been the one who died? Would he want Mia to be happy if it meant marrying another man?

Was someone pelting his chest with a mallet?

He pictured her the way he'd been for the past three years—lonely and burdened with bills and guilty with grief—and he exhaled, long and loud.

He'd want her to be happy. Even if it meant marrying someone else.

As the truck rolled along, he let his mind go.

What should I do? Will You help me?

Brittany reminded him what it felt like to be alive, to be accepted, to be valued.

Could he survive ten more years without her? Did he want to?

He would shrivel into a bitter, ugly man.

Brittany brought out the best in him. He couldn't take another ten years without her.

He needed her. And he was finally ready to accept it.

Chapter Fifteen

Hope and dread wound like ribbon around her throat. Brittany read the text twice.

Meet me at the tire swing in ten minutes.

She'd heard those exact words from Mason every weekday in the summer. As soon as he'd finish his ranch chores, he'd scarf down lunch and call her. She'd looked forward to his daily call more than she cared to admit.

And here she was, almost thirty years old, and the words still sent her pulse into a tizzy.

"I'm going out to the barn for a little bit, Nan," she called. It was still early in the morning. The Christmas Eve service was hours away.

"Okay, honey."

As she pulled on her coat and boots, she admired the Christmas tree. It filled the room with its fragrant scent. So much had changed since she'd arrived. How could it have been only last week that she and Mason and Noah had chopped it down?

She went out the front door and took her time getting to the barn. The fresh, crisp air kissed her cheeks.

Why did Mason want to meet her? He'd already made it as clear as the blue sky above he had no room for her in his heart.

Whatever he wanted to say, she'd hear him out. But she wasn't budging on moving here.

She looked around the land and couldn't wait to explore it again. The line of trees in the distance probably housed wildlife she didn't know about. A creek snaked around the other side of the ridge past the barn. Hot springs were within driving distance. When summer arrived, the rodeos would return, and she could practically taste the greasy food she used to buy at them.

If only Mason would share it all with her…

She'd stay out of his way. Keep an emotional distance, as well. It might kill her, but she'd respect his wishes.

Just because she'd fallen back in love in a matter of minutes didn't mean the feeling was mutual. And why would it be? His life was fuller than hers. He had a son and a wife he was mourning and a twin brother to get to know and an entire town who supported and loved him.

He didn't need her.

Not the way she needed him.

She'd been rash to unload her feelings on him yesterday.

The barn door slid open easily. The swing was the first thing she saw. She closed her eyes, remembering all the times she and Mason had shared their dreams, laughed at each other's jokes and just hung out together, content to be with each other.

Ten years of not having him… An inferno burned inside her to have those moments with him all over again.

Meow. One of the cats rubbed against her leg.

"Oh, kitty, you're hungry, aren't you?" She bent down to pet its ginger head. The cat began to purr. "Come on, let's get some food. I should have brought you a Christmas feast. I'll bring you leftover ham later, I promise."

She poured kibble into the dishes and filled the water bowls. After petting each cat, she checked her phone. Ten minutes had come and gone. And there was no sign of Mason.

Plunking down on a bale of hay, she watched the cats lick their paws and stretch.

Christmas Eve in a barn. Far away from her home in California…

She sniffed in amusement—not the same as Bethlehem, that was for sure. But the similarities made her smile. On a whim, she stood and did a pirouette, then she attempted a dance combo across the dirt floor. She chuckled and tore off her puffy jacket. Although winter boots didn't bring out her most graceful moves, she continued dancing.

Oh, Lord, thank You for taking my mind off you-know-who for a moment.

"I could watch you dance all day." Mason stood in the doorway, his shoulder against the frame.

She froze. Her heart jackhammered in her chest as he strode to her, confident, tall and intense. His eyes never left her face. And she recognized the aching need in them.

Don't get your hopes up. His eyes and his mouth might say two different things.

She tilted her chin to prepare for whatever he was about to say, but to her surprise, he didn't stop.

He scooped her into his arms and carried her to the swing. She couldn't protest—didn't know how.

Almost as soon as she was in his arms, he set her on the swing and knelt next to her. What was he doing? Being near him put a cloud of confusion over her thoughts.

His lips curved up in a tender smile. "Do you know

how many times over the years I wished I'd find you here?"

She shook her head, words refusing to form.

"I'd guess about a million, give or take." He took off his gloves and tossed them to the side. She could feel his warm breath on her face. He traced her cheek with the backs of his fingers. "I don't want to go another ten years without you."

Had she heard him correctly? Or was this a dream?

"You don't?" Her voice squeaked. Everything inside her—even the tips of her toes—tingled with anticipation.

He shook his head. "No. I've been pretty uptight for, let me see…" He lifted his gaze to the ceiling.

"Your entire life?" She easily fell into the teasing tone she reserved just for him.

"Yeah, I think that sums it up." His grin made him look younger, more carefree. "But when I'm with you, I feel more like me. It's hard to explain."

She knew exactly what he meant. When she was with him, she felt more like herself, too.

"I like who I am when I'm with you." He took her hand in his.

Her heart clenched. For years she hadn't been essential to anyone. To hear Mason say it…

"I like who you are," she said. "You're special, Mason. There's no one else like you."

"I don't know why you feel that way, Brit." He shook his head. "When it comes to you, I've been selfish. After high school I asked you to give up everything *you* wanted to fit into *my* world. It never even occurred to me to fit into yours. It was easy to blame you and your boyfriend back then. But you're right—he wasn't the real reason we broke up. You needed to go to college and chase your dreams. You wouldn't have been happy here."

She couldn't deny it. She *had* needed to go to college and experience the world for herself.

"I don't regret leaving." She kept her hands around the ropes, not trusting herself to let go. All she wanted to do was touch him. "I needed to figure out who I was."

"You're exactly who you were—but even better." His eyes gleamed. "And now you're actually willing to give up your life and dreams to be here—in my world. I threw it back in your face yesterday. Don't think I haven't spent every minute since then thinking about you. I have to ask you something, though. How do you feel when you're with me? Do you like who you are when I'm around?"

She frowned. What was he getting at? Of course she liked who she was when they were together.

"Is this a trick question?"

"No…" He tossed his head back. "I mean, after you're with me do you feel better or worse? Some people drain you. I don't want to be that guy."

She lowered her gaze. "I feel accepted. Known. But no, I don't always like who I am when I'm with you."

His expression darkened.

"I used to, Mason."

"I deserve that." He ducked his chin, nodding. "I thought the worst of you for years. I was awful—rude—when you showed up with Ryder. I accused you of not taking care of Nan. I can't imagine why you'd want anything to do with me. I've done nothing to earn your trust."

He wanted to reach out and catch the emotions dancing through her pretty blue eyes. He felt stripped of the things that made him who he was. With Mia, he'd felt he had a lot to offer—his love of ranching, family, a future. But with Brittany, he'd become keenly aware that none of his assets were things she cared about.

It would be a lopsided relationship with him taking all her goodness and giving little in return.

"That's not what I meant," she said gently. "When we were young, I felt full of life and pretty and exciting when I was with you. You accepted me as I was. And when I'm with you now, I can see my inadequacies. It's not because of anything you do or say."

"I'm sorry, Brittany. I don't mean to make you feel that way." He covered her small hands still clutching the ropes with his.

"There's nothing to apologize for. I see how you care for Nan. Day in, day out. I see the way you are with Noah. The responsibilities you never shirk. You're kind to your in-laws even when they're overbearing. You're paying off hospital debts and never complain about it. If anything, when I'm with you, I want to be more like you. You make me want to be better."

Once again, she'd blindsided him, but this time with grace and compassion and things he didn't deserve from her.

"You couldn't be better. You're already the best." He leaned in. "I don't want you to be anyone but who you already are. You're easy to be with—do you know how hard it is for me to be comfortable around people? But you fit in with everyone. And you're fun. You're kind. You care."

Teardrops glistened below her lashes.

"Don't cry. I don't want to upset you." He flicked a drop away with his thumb. "I'm only saying this because you're incredible, and I don't even think you know it."

"Mason, will you level with me?" Worried eyes met his. "Yes."

"Why are you saying all this? Last night you made it clear Mia was it for you. There was no room for me. Ever."

"I wasn't ready." He averted his gaze for a moment. "But today—well, a lot has happened today. I made peace with Mia. I talked to Bill. I even talked to the good Lord. I lost my parents and twin brother as an infant. I lost my grandparents as a young adult. I lost my wife way before I ever should have lost her. And I lost you once. I don't want to lose you again."

"What are you saying?" Her eyes glowed with hope.

"I'm saying I love you. I'm saying I want you to move to Rendezvous, and I want to get to know you all over again. I'll help you fix up the studio. If you need me to dress up like Jack Sparrow, I will. I'll do whatever you want, but please tell me you'll be mine."

He held his breath.

She looked shell-shocked, then she exhaled and everything changed. Her eyes crinkled in the corners and her lips curved into a wondrous smile.

"I'm yours." She wound her arms around his neck. "I've always been yours."

That was all he needed to hear. He leaned forward and pressed his lips to hers. She tasted like a summer dream. Sunshine and beach and bottled-up joy. He cradled her face in his hands and drank her in. This woman—they were meant to be together. Slowly, he ended the kiss.

"Oh, Mason…" They stared into each other's eyes. "I got an idea while watching *White Christmas* with Nan the other night."

"Oh yeah?" He couldn't tear his gaze from her lips.

"I think we should re-create the dance scene with the sisters."

"With the blue feathers?"

"Yeah." Her smile lit her face.

"I'm in." He'd prance around with blue feathers, slay a dragon—anything for her. "Can I ask why?"

"I don't know. It'll be fun." She shrugged, grinning.

"Good enough for me." He untangled himself from the swing and held out his hand. "Merry Christmas Eve."

"Merry Christmas Eve." A smirk lifted her lips. "Do me a favor."

"What?"

"Give me a push like you used to do."

He laughed. "Think you can handle it?"

She wiggled her eyebrows. He gave her a big push, and she squealed, leaning back until the swing slowed.

After she hopped off, he pulled her into his arms. Then he kissed her again. He thought ahead to all the afternoons they had to look forward to and not just in the summer, but all year long.

"Come on," she said, grabbing his hand. "Let's go tell Nan."

"Think she'll be happy?"

"I think she'll be ecstatic."

Chapter Sixteen

This was hands down the best day of her life.

The final strains of "Silent Night, Holy Night" rang through the sanctuary, and Brittany set her hand on Mason's arm. She sat between him and Nan. Next to Mason were Noah, Ryder, Harper and Ivy. Bill, Joanna and Eden sat in front of them, and Noah had poked Auntie Eden's back often, prompting Mason to scold him more than once during the service.

Thank You, Lord. Your plan was so much better than my own. You've done mighty things for me today.

She glanced over at Nan, who smiled and grew teary-eyed again. She'd cried tears of joy when Brittany and Mason told her they were in love. She'd brought her palms together, raised her gaze to the ceiling and assured them her prayers had been answered before kissing each of them on the cheek.

"Hi, Miss Bwittany," Noah whispered for the sixth time while he waved at her. She smiled, putting her finger to her lips, then waved back. When Mason had told Noah that Brittany was his girlfriend, Noah had hugged her so hard, she'd almost fallen over. Facing her, he'd sat on her lap and hugged her neck. Then he'd whispered in her ear that he wanted her to be his mommy.

It had been one of the sweetest moments in her life.

Mason had taken it upon himself to tell his in-laws and Eden in person, and afterward he'd called Gabby with the good news.

Brittany had the less inviting task of calling her mother. When she'd told Mom she was moving in with Nan and opening a studio in Rendezvous, her mother had responded with, "I hope you know what you're doing."

She and Nan had invited her to come out and spend some time with them, but she'd declined. At least Mom had wished Nan a merry Christmas.

An organ heartily pumped out "Joy to the World," while ushers marched to the front to excuse everyone.

"My Christmas gift is right here," Mason whispered to her. His eyes glimmered with love, and her breath caught in her throat.

"You didn't want chocolate-covered cherries?"

"I only want you."

Heat flushed up her neck. But the ushers were at their pew, so she helped Nan rise and hooked arms with her as they made their way down the aisle. Life had sure changed in twenty-four hours. God willing, from here on out, she'd be spending all her Christmases with Nan and Mason and Noah.

In the entryway, they were met with cries of "Merry Christmas" and lots of hugs. Bill and Joanna approached them.

"I hear you're moving to town, Brittany." Bill spoke kindly. Joanna wrung her hands.

"Yes, I'm excited to spend more time with Nan."

"We're very happy you'll be spending more time with Mason, too." Joanna tried to smile, and Brittany could see how much it was costing her. Pity stabbed her heart over this couple's loss.

"Welcome to Rendezvous." Bill held his arms out.

Was he offering to hug her? She'd been pretty sure he didn't like her. She moved forward into his arms and was surprised at how genuine the embrace felt.

"Thank you." She glanced at Joanna again. The woman was clearly trying to keep it together. Brittany put her arms around her. "I'm sorry. I'm sure the holidays must be hard, and I know my presence isn't helping."

A tear trailed down Joanna's cheek, but she smiled and whisked it away. "I miss Mia, but I'm very happy for you and Mason."

Eden picked up Noah. "Are you ready for presents tomorrow?"

He nodded, holding her neck tightly. "Yes! Auntie Eden, did you know Miss Bwittany is Daddy's girlfriend?"

"I heard that." Eden rubbed his little back. "It's wonderful news."

Brittany locked eyes with her and Eden smiled.

"Do you think Ivy will get the doll she wants?" Noah snuggled into Eden's arms.

"I certainly hope she does." She brushed his hair from his forehead.

"Me, too."

Gabby came over and tapped Brittany's shoulder. "I hear you're moving to Rendezvous."

"I am." She liked Gabby and Eden and hoped they'd all be friends. "I'm buying the old computer repair shop."

"Good for you. It will be great having you around." Gabby looked at Eden, then Mason, who stood next to Brittany. "While you're all here, I have my own announcement."

"I'll just get Nan's coat," Brittany said, wanting to give them privacy.

"Stay," Gabby said. "You're one of us now."

One of them. Of all the nice things to say... Brittany's emotions couldn't take much more.

"I might have done something stupid." Gabby lifted her palm. "Seeing that it's Christmas, I sent one final letter to Phoebe's father. But I'm holding firm from now on. I'm not going to try to contact him anymore."

"You've done more than most would in this situation." Eden put her arm around Gabby's shoulders and squeezed.

"Thanks, Eden."

Brittany knew Gabby was raising her sister's baby, but she hadn't realized the father was an issue. It wasn't any of her business, but she would be glad to lend a hand whenever Gabby needed one.

"We'll support whatever decision you make," Mason said.

"Brittany!" Babs O'Rourke wove through the crowd. "Oh, I'm glad I caught you. Merry Christmas, honey."

"Merry Christmas." She was taken aback at her red-and-white-striped blazer with red skirt. She looked like a walking candy cane.

"I'll have the papers drawn up the day after tomorrow. Will you be in town?"

"Yes, I will." She and Babs discussed the property for a few more minutes while Mason chatted with his friends.

After Babs left, Brittany took a moment to savor it all. Nan stood with Lois and Gretchen. Bill and Joanna were fussing over Noah, still in Eden's arms. Ryder was twirling Harper, then Ivy, who both giggled with glee. Mason locked eyes with Brittany and smiled.

Who would have thought all her dreams could come true in a middle-of-nowhere town?

She strolled over to Mason. This was where she belonged.

Epilogue

It was going to be another awesome summer.

Mason tripped on a toy dinosaur and landed on a plastic horse with his bare foot. *Ouch!* He counted to three as the pain subsided. Noah was kicking off the first day of June at Grandma and Grandpa Page's. Bill was teaching him how to ride a sheep for the Mutton Bustin' event at the rodeo, and Joanna promised to fill him up with a gooey ice cream sundae afterward. Which left Mason alone, contemplating when Brittany would get here already.

So much had changed since Christmas, and all of it for the better. After much prayer, he'd accepted Bill and Joanna's generous gift and paid off every medical bill. The ranch was thriving again, and his relationship with his in-laws was, too.

A knock on the front door made his heartbeat go faster.

He loped over and threw it open. To long blond hair and ocean-blue eyes. To sunshine and happiness. To his new bride, Brittany Fanning.

He hauled her into his arms and twirled her in a circle. Then he kissed her.

"What took you so long?" He pressed his forehead to

hers and she laughed. They'd gotten married a week ago, taken a short honeymoon in Yellowstone, and tonight, Brittany was moving her things into his house.

"Ahem?"

Mason looked over at the man standing next to her. The man who looked exactly like him. Ryder was back in town.

"Look who I ran into. And I didn't even splash coffee all over myself this time." She hitched her thumb at Ryder. "I thought we could use some extra help with moving boxes."

He gave Ryder a half hug. Ryder had been his best man at the wedding. It felt as if they'd been best friends forever. "What brings you back so soon?"

"Lily has the girls, so I figured I'd help you move." Sadness and pain lurked beneath his smile. "I'm staying at the inn, though. Don't want to cramp you newlyweds."

"I'm glad you're here." Mason held up a finger. "Let me get my boots on, and we'll start getting my new bride settled."

As soon as the boots were on, he went back out to the porch. Another car pulled up the driveway, and Gabby and Eden got out.

"Hey, we thought you might need a couple more hands." Gabby held up a plate of goodies. "And brownies."

Eden faltered when she saw Ryder, but she gave him a polite smile and came inside.

"Did someone say brownies?" Brittany rushed forward. "Who's watching Phoebe?"

"Babs insisted. She just loves the child." Gabby pulled off the cling wrap, and Brittany and Eden both took a treat. "She kind of adopted us both. I'm thankful for her, and not just because of her help with Phoebe. Babs has been running interference for me with a certain church lady. Gretchen won't get off my back about dating Judd. Babs, thankfully, has told her time and again I will not date a cowboy. Period."

"Isn't Judd technically a rancher?" Brittany took a bite of brownie as Mason shimmied next to her and put his arm around her waist. "Mmm…so good."

"Don't we get brownies?" Mason pointed to Ryder and himself.

"Yes, you get brownies." Gabby rolled her eyes and held out the plate. He and Ryder took the biggest ones.

"How is your grandmother doing?" Eden asked Brittany.

"Really well. I know it will be another transition with me moving out, but Vera Wick has been such a blessing. I'm so glad we hired her when I first moved back. Nan's used to her coming over a few times a week to help her shower and clean her house, so I don't think me moving down the road will be too bad. I'll pop in and see her every day. It's a win-win."

"If you need help, just let us know." Eden touched Brittany's arm.

"Thanks."

"Just so you know, Nicole has been having back pains," Gabby said, widening her eyes. "I hope the babies don't come early."

Mason felt terrible for Nicole Taylor, Stella Boone's sister. Her husband had died on Christmas day, and she'd moved back to Rendezvous and was staying with her mom and Stella. The worst part was that Nicole was pregnant with triplets. He could imagine how devastated she felt. He'd been in her shoes—not with triplets, but being overwhelmed with grief and trying to raise a baby without Mia. He and Gabby and Eden had promptly invited her to join their support group, and to their relief, she'd been coming to the Tuesday meetings for a few months.

"She went to the clinic," Eden said. "It must not be too serious. I mean, they sent her home."

"We'll keep praying for her," Mason said.

"Now that you're married, have you changed your mind about coming to our meetings, Brittany?" Gabby asked.

Brittany laughed. "I appreciate the offer. Thank you, but when summer's over I'll be teaching second and third graders tap that night. Until then, I'll keep hanging out with my little Noah-bear while you guys do your thing."

"I could use a group like yours," Ryder muttered. Then, as if he realized he'd said it out loud, his cheeks grew red and he shook his head. "Sorry."

"Well, if you lived here, we'd love to have you." Gabby covered the brownies with the plastic wrap.

"Maybe I'll have to move here." Ryder glanced at Eden. She proceeded to stare at the ground.

"Okay, where do we start?" Gabby asked.

"I have a bunch of boxes in the back of Nan's truck."

Ryder, Gabby and Eden strolled out to the truck, but Mason took Brittany's hand to hold her back.

"I love you, you know." He looked into her eyes and got a surge of anticipation at all the mischief and love in them.

"Prove it." She lifted her chin.

"Those are fighting words." He twirled her, then caught her up close to him. He slid his hands down her back to settle at her waist. Then he kissed her, savoring the promise of forever on her lips. "Now that the studio is remodeled and the apartment is renovated, you'll have more free time on your hands."

"I will." She wound her arms around his neck. "You know what that means?"

"No." He couldn't tear his gaze from her mouth.

"You're not going to be able to get rid of me." She lifted on tippy-toes and pressed her lips to his.

"Why would I want to? I'll never be able to get enough of you."

"Good, because I'm never going to let you go."

* * * * *

*Watch for the next book in
Jill Kemerer's Wyoming Sweethearts miniseries,
coming in Spring 2020!*

Dear Reader,

What's better than a new cowboy series set in Wyoming? I had so much fun dreaming up Rendezvous. I could picture the river running through town, the mountains nearby and the cute downtown full of restaurants and shops to be featured in all four of the books. And as the setting jelled in my mind, the people in it came to life.

I've cried many tears over Mason and his loss. And Brittany...how many times did I want to hug her and tell her how wonderful she is? So many people walk through life not realizing how much they have to offer the world. They're so much more than their job title or bank account balance. Mason needed Brittany's brightness and acceptance, and she needed his steadiness and devotion.

Could you relate to Brittany's realization that she would never find her identity in the things of this world? Her identity rests in being God's beloved child. Every now and then, I forget this, too, but thankfully, God gently reminds me I'm His and I don't need to be more.

Thank you, again, for reading my book!

Blessings to you,
Jill Kemerer

WE HOPE YOU ENJOYED THIS BOOK!

Love Inspired®

New beginnings. Happy endings.
Discover uplifting inspirational
romance.

Look for six new Love Inspired
books available every month,
wherever books are sold!

LoveInspired.com

AVAILABLE THIS MONTH FROM
Love Inspired®

AN AMISH CHRISTMAS PROMISE
Green Mountain Blessings • by Jo Ann Brown
Carolyn Wiebe will do anything to protect her late sister's children from their abusive father—even give up her Amish roots and pretend to be Mennonite. But when she starts falling for Amish bachelor Michael Miller, can they conquer their pasts—and her secrets—by Christmas to build a forever family?

COURTING THE AMISH NANNY
Amish of Serenity Ridge • by Carrie Lighte
Embarrassed by an unrequited crush, Sadie Dienner travels to Maine to take a nanny position for the holidays. But despite her vow to put romance out of her mind, the adorable little twins and their handsome Amish father, Levi Swarey, soon have her wishing for love.

THE RANCHER'S HOLIDAY HOPE
Mercy Ranch • by Brenda Minton
Home to help with his sister's wedding, Max St. James doesn't plan to stay past the holidays. With wedding planner Sierra Lawson pulling at his heartstrings, though, he can't help but wonder if the small town he grew up in is right where he belongs.

THE SECRET CHRISTMAS CHILD
Rescue Haven • by Lee Tobin McClain
Back home at Christmastime with a dark secret, single mom Gabby Hanks needs a job—and working at her high school sweetheart's program for at-risk kids is the only option. Can she and Reese Markowski overcome their past...and find a second chance at a future together?

HER COWBOY TILL CHRISTMAS
Wyoming Sweethearts • by Jill Kemerer
The last people Mason Fanning expects to find on his doorstep are his ex-girlfriend Brittany Green and the identical twin he never knew he had. Could this unexpected Christmas reunion bring the widower and his little boy the family they've been longing for?

STRANDED FOR THE HOLIDAYS
by Lisa Carter
All cowboy Jonas Stone's little boy wants for Christmas is a mother. So when runaway bride AnnaBeth Cummings is stranded in town by a blizzard, the local matchmakers are sure she'd make the perfect wife and mother. But can they convince the city girl to fall for the country boy?

LIATMBPA1219

"You won't have to stay on our account, and we can look after Ernest's place, too. I can hire a man to help me. Someone I know I can…" Ruth's words trailed away.

Trust? Depend on? Was that what Ruth was going to say? She didn't want him around. She couldn't have made it any clearer. Maybe it had been a mistake to think he could patch things up between them, but he wasn't willing to give up after only one day. Ruth was nothing if not stubborn, but he could be stubborn, too.

Owen leaned back and chuckled.

"What's so funny?"

"I'm here until Ernest returns, Ruth. You can't get rid of me with a few well-placed insults."

She huffed and turned her back to him. "I didn't insult you."

"Ah, but you wanted to. I'd like to talk about my plans in the morning."

Ruth nodded. "You know my feelings, but I agree we both need to sleep on it."

Owen picked up his coat and hat, and left for his uncle's farm. The wind was blowing harder and the snow was piling up in growing drifts. It wasn't a fit night out for man nor beast. As if to prove his point, he found Meeka, Ernest's big guard dog, lying across the corner of the porch out of the wind. Instead of coming out to greet him, she whined repeatedly.

He opened the door of the house. "Come in for a bit." She didn't get up. Something was wrong. Was she hurt? He walked toward her. She sat up and growled low in her throat. She had never done that to him before. "Are you sick, girl?"

She looked back at something in the corner and whined softly. Over the wind he heard what sounded like a sobbing child. "What have you got there, Meeka? Let me see."

He came closer. There was a child in an Amish bonnet and bulky winter coat trying to bury herself beneath Meeka's thick fur. Where had she come from? Why was she here? He looked around. Where were her parents?

Don't miss
The Hope *by Patricia Davids,*
available now wherever
HQN™ books and ebooks are sold.

HQNBooks.com